D0482233

DEAR FRIENDS

Also by Lisa Greenwald

The Friendship List Series

The TBH Series

DEAR FRIENDS

LISA GREENWALD

KT KATHERINE TEGEN BOOKS
An Imprint of HarperCollins Publishers

Katherine Tegen Books is an imprint of HarperCollins Publishers.

Dear Friends
Copyright © 2022 by Lisa Greenwald

All rights reserved. Printed in the United States of America.
No part of this book may be used or reproduced in any manner
whatsoever without written permission except in the case of brief
quotations embodied in critical articles and reviews. For information
address HarperCollins Children's Books, a division of HarperCollins
Publishers, 195 Broadway, New York, NY 10007.
www.harpercollinschildrens.com

Library of Congress Control Number: 2021950879
ISBN 978-0-06-306267-2

Typography by Molly Fehr
22 23 24 25 26 PC/LSCH   10 9 8 7 6 5 4 3 2 1

First Edition

In loving and everlasting memory of my mother,
Jo Ann Greenwald, who always wanted to know if
a new acquaintance was "best friend material."

"SYLVIE REBECCA BANK!"

I'm outside on the porch picking at a piece of banana bread from my favorite Longport bakery, actually called Banana Bread, when I see Sylvie walking up the path to my house. Her dirty-blond curls bounce against her shoulders. My heart feels like Pop Rocks when I see her, like we've been apart for years and years, not just two months. Us being back together—that makes my world feel complete again.

I put down my plate and run down the steps to meet her. "Eep! I'm so happy to see you." Pontoon follows behind me; this shih tzu always wants to be included. I wrap my arms around Sylvie's neck and we stay in an awkward, about-to-get-sweaty hug.

"Hi, Len," she says when we pull apart, not cheerful-sounding but not grumpy-sounding either. Somewhere in the middle. "Hi, Tuney Tune-Tunes."

She reaches down to pet him and he stands up and licks her knee.

We walk back to the porch together and sit on the rocking chairs and Sylvie looks at me, sort of seeming suspicious. "Your hair is so curly, did you sleep in braids or something?"

"Nope." I hold a few strands in my hand and inspect them. "I think it looks the same wavy brown it always does." I shrug. "I missed you so much, Sylv!" I have this overwhelming need to tell her everything right away, every single detail about what happened at camp with Maddy and how I felt so alone, but I feel like I need to wait. I don't want to start our first after-camp hang on such a sad note.

"I missed you, too," she answers, sort of flat.

We're silent then, like somehow we forgot how to talk to each other. I read somewhere that you actually have more to talk about with someone you talk to all the time. When you don't talk for a while, there's less to say, even though you'd think it would be the opposite.

"What's with these binders?" she asks, looking at the porch floor. "Ooh, that looks like my handwriting!"

"It is your handwriting." I laugh. "I'm doing the thing I always do when I get home from camp. Putting the letters

I sent home in one binder and the letters I got in another binder, archived forever." I roll my eyes. "You know how my mom is."

"Right, yeah." She leans back in the chair. "You didn't really write me as much this summer, though."

My face turns hot for a second. "Well, it was kind of a hard summer. Remember my friend Maddy?" I ask her.

"Um." She thinks for a second. "Not really."

I feel a little surprised that she doesn't remember. "Well, she got super obsessed with soccer and pretty much stopped hanging out with me and I was stuck with these other girls who were fine but not my favorite." I pause. "I'm so grateful to be home with you now, and so excited to hang with everyone and just get ready for middle school together."

Sylvie nods and stretches her legs out in front of her. "Yeah, I mean, I hung out with Annie and Paloma all summer pretty much. You may not get all of our jokes and stuff, no offense." I ignore the all-over body sting I feel when she says that. "I mean, we hung out, like, every single day. It was mostly Annie and Paloma, though, since Zora was at her grandma's in Maryland for half the summer, but sometimes Zora was there, too." She pauses. "We called ourselves APS. Like appetizers."

"Or applications," I suggest. "Like on a phone?"

"That too. Yeah." Sylvie giggles. "But when Zora was there, we were ZAPS."

I nod and force a smile. I wonder if there's room for my E in their acronym. ZAPES has a catchy ring to it.

Sylvie goes on. "I hung out with Anjali sometimes, too, after art class, but not that much. She was on this road trip with her parents for a while. They rented an RV!"

"Wow." My eyes bulge. "That sounds pretty awesome."

"Yeah. Paloma and I became super close, though," she muses, and I try not to feel that twitchy-heart feeling—the one I got a lot over the summer when Maddy was with Wren and Hattie and the other soccer girls all the time.

"Oh, fun," I say, trying to find some enthusiasm. "What'd you guys do together?"

"Went to the beach mostly. Oh! And we made all these new varieties of s'mores on her firepit—like check this out. One Oreo, one Chips Ahoy!, and then a marshmallow and a piece of chocolate."

"Wow," I say again.

"And we did *soo* many combinations like that. With all the different Oreo flavors." She goes on and on and I start to zone out a little bit.

"Very cool." I pick off another tiny crumb of banana bread. I want to finish it because it's so good, but suddenly my stomach is tangled up like computer wires. "Such a fun summer. I feel bummed that mine wasn't so great. And this Maddy thing was totally out of the blue. I still don't really understand it."

"Yeah. That's weird." She pauses. "Um, Anyway." She folds her hands on her lap, almost like she's waiting for me to say something, but I'm still tied up from all the Paloma talk and the s'mores varieties. I feel left out of something I was never going to be part of in the first place. "So can we please talk about my birthday party? I know it's our tradition to start planning as soon as you're home from camp, but it was really hard for me to wait that long this year."

"Yes, but first!" I do a little drum roll on my lap, feeling relieved I can bring something fun into this bummer conversation. "I have the best best best idea for our costume for the sixth-grade overnight."

"Oh yeah?" Sylvie asks. "Did you already add it to the list of our costume ideas? I can't believe we've been talking about this since third grade!"

"I didn't add it yet, but if you like it, I will." I turn to face her a little bit. "A bar of soap and a loofah! Two counselors wore it for Masquerade Night at camp and it was so awesome."

"Really?" Sylvie asks, her face scrunched. "I don't know. That feels weird, Len. No offense."

I scratch the back of my head. "Well, it was just an idea. Anyway, we still have time."

"So now can we please please please brainstorm my party?" Sylvie claps and gets a notebook and a pen out of her Longport Cones (only the best ice cream shop in the history of ice cream) tote bag. She smiles a cheery smile and I push my left-out feelings away. Maybe all the Maddy stuff seeped into my brain and made me overly sensitive to the ZAPS talk.

Sylvie's here, like always, and we're planning her birthday party, like always. Everything's fine. So what that she wasn't into my idea? I mean, maybe soap and loofah feels too personal, even in costume form.

"Yes! Ready to rock!" I raise my hands in the air, mimicking my counselor Natalie from camp this summer. "First tell me all of your ideas, so I know what you're already thinking."

"A backyard thing for sure 'cause my s'mores summer was so magical. And since September is still so warm. I kind of just want to extend summer as much as I can." She pauses. "So like backyard movie night?"

"Oooh! Yes! You can order those little containers of popcorn. Maybe even rent a real popcorn machine," I suggest.

"Yes! Brilliant!" She claps, all excited.

"Guest list?" I ask, staring at a squirrel who keeps running up and down the same tree.

"Obviously Annie and Paloma. Zora. You. Anjali and maybe the other girls I'm friends with from art class." She pauses. "Maybe Liam and Patrick from across the street? I don't know. They're going to Catholic Middle School, so we won't see them so much anymore. And should I make this a boys-girls thing or no?"

"Hmmm." I think for a moment. "All girls."

We're eleven now (almost twelve, in Sylvie's case) and it doesn't feel as easy to be friends with boys as it used to.

"But what about Rumi and Elizabeth?" I ask. "You're friends with them too even if they're not your best best best friends, know what I mean? But since they're best friends with Anjali it kind of overlaps."

"I guess." She pauses, seeming a little annoyed I'm bringing this up. "But I'm not close with them at all, we never hang out outside of school, and I need to invite Callie and the twins from my art class. I saw them once a week, all summer."

"Okay." I want to mention that it may be weird when we're back at school and Rumi and Elizabeth find out they weren't invited, but I stop myself.

Sylvie writes down all the names and it comes to nine, including her, which feels like the right amount for a backyard movie night. Her backyard is big but not that big and we wouldn't want it to feel crowded or chaotic.

"Oh!" I yelp. "I just remembered something."

"What?"

"This girl in my bunk at camp—Shir—she was new this summer and kind of an annoying braggy type, but anyway, she did this thing for her birthday last year—and she told us about it and it seemed so awesome at the time that I meant to write to you about it but then I forgot." I pause to catch my breath. "Anyway, she rented these teeny tiny tents for her birthday! In the backyard! This lady, the owner of the company, comes to set it up and everything and they come with string lights and pillows and little tables and it was seriously the coolest ever."

Sylvie's eyes widen like it's the best thing she's ever heard. "Really? Can you find out the name of it? Can you ask her? I really want to do this!"

"Yes, yes, and yes!" I pick up my phone and then realize I don't have Shir's number stored in my phone. I'll need to look it up when I go inside. "I'll do it right after you leave."

I don't know why it took me so long to remember this, but it's truly the finishing touch for this party, the cherry on the sundae (even though I hate cherries). I mean— twelve is big. It feels old. Plus, it's the last birthday before we're teenagers. And Sylvie's is always the first party of the school year so that's also a big deal, too. A kickoff, basically.

"Len! I am so so so excited." We stand up and she reaches over and hugs me and it feels like a real true BFF hug, not awkward at all, the way it was before. "I need to go home because my mom promised she'd take me back-to-school shopping today since we're leaving for

Block Island with my cousins tomorrow. Can you let me know ASAP when you hear back from Shir so I can ask my mom?" She gets up and picks a wedgie and straightens out the legs of her cuffed pink shorts.

"Are ZAP home this week to hang out with me?" I laugh.

"Um." Sylvie raises her eyebrows. "Way to jump in our joke."

That stings, but I think she's kidding. This isn't a big deal.

"JK. But no, they're not really. Paloma is doing that camping trip she always does with the families from church and I think Zora's going back to her grandma's."

I nod. "What about Annie?"

"Oh, she's not gonna be able to hang. They're renovating their whole house because the basement flooded last week and so she has to help her mom pack up and stuff."

"Oh, wow. That sounds hectic." I pick up Pontoon and snuggle him close. I guess he'll be my buddy for the week.

"It is sooooo hectic but it's gonna be amazing when it's done. You know how Annie's house has always been kinda tight for them; it's really small."

"I guess?" I've never thought that much about Annie's house before.

"Well, there's going to be this awesome finished basement now and they're getting a Ping-Pong table and a pinball machine and this huge couch where we can hang out and have sleepovers and stuff." She pauses. "Anyway, gotta go, so excited for middle school!"

Sylvie starts walking down the path and I yell, "Countdown to the sixth-grade overnight is OFFICIALLY ON!"

She turns around and looks at me weird, like maybe my excitement is over the top, but then she smiles and gives me a thumbs-up and keeps walking home.

I swallow hard. I really hope ZAPES can be a thing.

I SPEND THE LAST WEEK of summer vacation doing homework. So sad, but true.

Sylvie was right that no one was around and I'm trying not to get too bogged down by the fact that everyone's away or busy and that I haven't seen Annie or Paloma or Zora or anyone else since I got home.

Once we have Sylvie's party this weekend and school gets going, things will be normal and I'll be back into the groove with everyone.

Sometimes my brain goes down a worry spiral, though, that what happened at camp with Maddy will happen at school, too. I try to drag that thought to the trash can of my brain, the way I'd do with a document on my laptop.

I'm on shaky ground now, but once school starts and I get into the swing of middle school, I'll feel okay again.

For our summer homework, we had to complete a horrible math packet, and read three books, and we also had to write an essay about our name. Everyone was so annoyed about it, saying it was dumb. But I'll be honest— I was excited about it. I think it's because I love my name.

Everyone calls me Len or Leni but my real name is Eleni.

Eleni Belle Klarstein to be exact.

Eleni is for my grandmother Helen, my mom's mom, who I didn't know but have heard so much about. She died a few months before I was born, and my mom was super close to her. It was one of those rare tragedies you read about and you feel so terrible after and then you remind yourself over and over again to tell your loved ones that you love them because life is fleeting and unpredictable and all that.

Eleni is a variation on Helen and they both mean bright, shining light in Greek. We're not Greek but the meaning is amazing, especially since I was afraid of the dark until I was eight. And my middle name Belle is for my great-grandmother, Helen's mom, Annabelle.

So basically I have the whole essay written already in my head, but I do need to get it down on paper. We have to type all our assignments, but I always write first drafts in my journal first. My journal is basically an extension of my brain.

It makes sense because my ultimate dream in life is to own a stationery store when I'm older. The last name I came up with was Len's Pens (And More) but I'm not one hundred percent in love with it. I think I can do better, and thankfully I have time to think of something amazing.

I'm on the hammock, listening to the audiobook of *One Crazy Summer* by Rita Williams-Garcia when it stops abruptly because I have a FaceTime call from Sylvie.

"Hi! Just wanted to tell you we booked the tent lady! My mom looked it up online and found it right before you texted with the info from Shir."

"Oh! Great!"

"Yes! So excited. Lucky she was free since it was last minute! I can't believe—" The call cuts out then, probably from bad cell service on the island, and her words are garbled for a few more minutes and then the call drops entirely. I try a few more times to reach her after that but eventually give up and go back to my audiobook.

"Len, are you doing the summer homework?" my mom calls from inside. "I hate to have to nag you about it."

"About to get started," I shout back.

Pontoon looks up at me, dubious. If a dog can tell I'm not telling the truth, it must be pretty obvious.

"Tuney Tune-Tunes," I whisper. "I'll get started soon. Don't worry."

He follows behind me as I run inside and up to my

room to get my journal and my favorite fine-tip gel pen.

"You're still not working?" my mom yaps at me as I run past her to go back outside. "Len, come on, please. I hate nagging."

I sigh and try not to get aggravated. My mom kind of nags a lot for someone who says she hates it!

It's part of her anxiety, I think, always wanting everything to be just so, a certain way, the best it can be. She likes to control things—not just specific things, pretty much anything, everything, all the things.

That's why her job as the executive director at Monterey Springs, *Middleport's finest senior living community*, really works for her. She gets to be in charge and everyone loves her for it.

"I'm going outside to do the summer assignments," I sing, and grab a mini can of Sprite on my way out the door. "Don't worry."

I sit down at the table on the deck, and Pontoon curls up under my chair.

I uncap the pen, about to start writing my name essay, but then the Maddy brain spiral comes back and the only way to get rid of it is to jot down my thoughts.

I can't stop thinking about this whole Maddy thing; it's always there, in the back of my brain, lingering like the musty smell in a basement. It won't go away. And I don't know what to do or who to talk to.

I try to retrace the steps a little. Like this happened and then that happened kind of thing.

We got to camp and things were normal, eating brown sugar from the yogurt bar for breakfast the way we do every summer, and Maddy was on the top bunk and I was on the bottom like always. And then little by little, things were different. She didn't wait for me to walk down to dinner. She didn't want to sign up for pottery elective with me. She wasn't mean, but she felt far away all the time.

She always wanted to be with Wren and Hattie and the rest of the soccer girls. And I kept thinking—okay, but at least she's with me when we're in the bunk, like at rest hour, at least she writes letters on my bed like always, at least we walk back from canteen together. But then little by little those things stopped, too, and everything felt strained and confusing and it was hard to remember a time when she was my camp best friend.

I ended up hanging out with Lilia and Shir a lot because they were new and didn't have anyone else and I guess I eventually didn't either.

I need to stop writing. Too painful. Bye for now.

I close my journal and get up from the table, feeling an overwhelming need to close my eyes.

I walk over to the hammock; just ten more minutes of relaxing and then I'll get to work. For real.

Me: Sooooo excited for your party!

Me: Deciding between my gingham romper and my overall shorts

Me: Do you have time for a super quick FaceTime to help me pick?

Sylvie doesn't text me back; I guess she's busy setting up for the party. After Sylvie got back from Block Island, I was waiting for her to bring up a time to do a FaceTime fashion show to plan our outfits for the party, and when she didn't, I felt weird suggesting it.

I take selfies to try and get a sense of how I look, then I fall down a rabbit hole rereading journal entries about past years' parties. I think that's the best part of keeping a journal—being able to reread and remember stuff I'd probably have forgotten. I guess I shouldn't eye roll so much about my mom documenting everything, since I kinda do it, too.

Being a saver is probably genetic.

After the party at the arcade, I went back to Sylvie's for a sleepover. As we were falling asleep that night, Sylvie said my present was her favorite. I knew that rhinestone mini backpack was awesome the moment I saw it!

I flip all the way back to the beginning of this journal to see how old I was when I started this particular book.

Eleni & Sylvie's Mission to get our moms to let us get our ears pierced on the last day of third grade.

- Be as polite as we can
- Never complain about what's for dinner
- Always compliment our moms on their earrings
- Research best places in Longport for ear piercing
- Ask them super nicely if we can please go together

I crack up so much about this because we were completely obsessed and we kept bringing it up over and over to our moms, begging them, and nothing was working.

I remember the day we came up with this mission. So vividly, too. We were in Sylvie's backyard on the loungers on her patio, feeling defeated. The mission made us feel better immediately. And our moms were, like, over-the-top impressed. It showed we were taking responsibility for something we really, really wanted.

I want to text her about this, but it feels weird to text so many times without her writing back, and she's getting ready for the party anyway.

After a few more minutes debating my outfit, I decide on denim overall shorts with my faded gray tee and I'll bring my navy hoodie, since it's going to get chilly. We're in that part of the year when the air wants to remind us that the best part of summer is behind us. The sun sets earlier, the air is crisper, fall is about to be here and it wants to make its appearance known.

Maybe fall feels jealous of summer. I wonder if fall thinks to itself: *I'm good too. I have Halloween and cider doughnuts and apple picking. I'm good too! Please love me!*

I run down the stairs and find my mom reading on the couch in the den. "Ready to go?" I ask her. I could walk to Sylvie's on my own, of course, since it's only three blocks away, but my mom has to run an errand anyway so she said she'd drive me.

"Yup." She smiles.

My dad is on the back deck grilling salmon and bok choy in his LakeLife apron, the one with the kayaks on it.

My mom got it for his birthday a few years ago. He grew up in a little woodsy lake community in Massachusetts and still really misses it. My dad's dad, my grandfather, had the job of cleaning the lake every morning from May to October, literally driving a big orange boat around, sucking up all the muck from the lake and keeping it clean for the residents. They were among the few who lived there year-round; most of the others were summer people.

When we get to Sylvie's house, there's a huge lawn sign that says HAPPY BIRTHDAY SYLVIE in rainbow letters. I grab the present from the trunk (a denim jacket with patches of many of her favorite things—music notes, a rainbow, a peace sign, hearts, and a giant sun). When we bought it, I loved it so much that I begged my mom to get a similar one for me.

Sylvie loves to match so I bet we'll plan to both wear them on the same day sometimes.

"Bye, Mom."

"Bye, Len. I'll pick you up at nine."

"K. Enjoy the salmon."

"Have fun, okay?"

I close the door, a little confused. What does that even mean? Of course I'll have fun. It's a party.

I walk around the back, through the wrought iron gate, and Zora's the first person I see. She's tying balloons on all the chairs. Sylvie's dad is adjusting the huge outdoor movie screen and Taylor Swift is playing, not blasting levels, more like background music.

No one sees me at first; I hate that feeling. You want to walk into a place and be greeted immediately. Like, "Hey, Eleni!" Of course, you also want a "Yay! You're here! The party can start now" too, but it's not necessary. But the feeling when you walk into a place and no one notices you at first—that's no good. It sets the whole party off on an uneven seesaw kind of thing. Like you'll have to make up for lost time, reset, push down all the soggy-bread feelings until you feel okay again.

I walk over to Zora tying the balloons, since Sylvie's not out here yet. Maybe she's still getting ready.

"Hi, Zora," I say, pulling down one leg of my overall shorts. I gently place the gift bag with Sylvie's present on the wicker love seat in the corner of her deck.

"Oh, hi, Len." She smiles but doesn't reach out for a hug. But maybe we're not huggers. Did we used to hug? I can't even remember now.

"How was your summer?" I ask.

"Fine." She shrugs. "Nothing crazy. I was at my grandma's a lot. Yours?"

"Um, fine, too." I shove my hands in my pockets.

"Only fine? But you usually loooove camp," she says, confused-sounding.

"Yeah, it was good. I dunno. It was fun."

Zora hesitates a second and then says, "Sylvie's inside.

She's changed outfits like a hundred times. You know how she is."

I laugh. "Yeah, of course. It's kind of a miracle she ever shows up dressed for school."

"Huh?" She gives me a weird look.

"I mean, like, since she can't decide on outfits. Not like she'd come to school naked." I giggle.

"Oh. Um. Yeah."

"Can I help tie some balloons?" I ask her, feeling an urgent need for something to do.

"Sure. Go grab some from over there." She points to the corner of the deck where there's a giant black trash bag.

As I'm walking over, Sylvie comes out of her house, arms linked with Annie and Paloma. They're wearing matching mint-green tank tops and denim skirts with frayed edges. Paloma's and Sylvie's are short but Annie's is long, of course. She is the queen of long skirts. They all have their hair in pigtail braids.

Did they plan to match? They must have. But Zora's not matching. She's in one of her favorite spaghetti-strap sundresses. And I'm realizing they must have all gotten here early to help set up, but Sylvie didn't ask *me* to come early.

My throat stings like I ate a still-on-fire roasted marshmallow about to be smooshed into a s'more. Suddenly it seems I don't belong here and I hate these overall shorts.

I feel like I'm dressed like a toddler.

"Happy birthday, Sylvie!" I yell, way too loud and way more cheerful than I actually feel. The words are clumsy and awkward falling out of my mouth.

"Thank you, Len." She smiles.

My heart inflates a little because when people call me Len, I get an overwhelming sense that things are actually fine, normal, happy, like there's nothing to worry about.

I keep tying balloons to the chairs and Zora does too, but Paloma, Annie, and Sylvie dance around like the party is really for the three of them, not for Sylvie's birthday. I want them to stop. I don't even know what they're doing exactly but I just want them to stop.

When Sylvie said she spent all summer with them, I figured it was like it always is when I'm away at camp. They go to the beach and the pool and to Longport Cones, and have family barbecues and movie nights and stuff, but then when I get home, it's all back to normal: Sylvie and Eleni BFFs like it's been forever, since the beginning of time.

We're part of the rest of the group, of course. But really, it's the two of us who are the center, the core of it all.

It doesn't seem like that now. It feels like something shifted and I wasn't prepared, or warned, or ready.

My stomach sinks. No no no. I don't like this. I want it to stop.

I had this worry, and it's almost like I willed it to happen; it's actually coming true. This is the ugly, opposite upside down of when you wish-wish-wish for something to happen, and then it actually does.

There are a few balloons left to put up, so I do that and then I try to sort of inch myself closer to Sylvie, Paloma, and Annie. It's like there's bubble wrap around them, or an electric fence like some people have for dogs. I get close and then I feel an invisible string pulling me away again.

They're dancing around and throwing their heads back, laughing constantly like everything is the funniest.

"Seriously," Paloma says in response to everything Annie says.

Zora and I are with them but not totally with them. We're off to the side just far enough that we feel like two different groups. The air feels thick all of a sudden, like we're stuck and can't move. I scan my brain for something to say but it's blank. I can't think of a single thing. I look at Zora to try to figure out how she's feeling.

"I'm over them," Zora whispers to me a few seconds later, as we finish tying the few balloons that are left. "They're not even fun anymore."

"They're not?" My voice is scratchy.

"Do they look fun to you?" she asks, her words harsh and cutting.

I glance in that direction and I want to say that yeah, they do look fun and I'm sad I'm not over there laughing with them, and that I want to be right in the center of it and I don't know why I'm not. That is where I should be.

Zora doesn't really wait for me to respond. "Anyway, I'm just so excited for middle school so I'll be with different people in all of my classes, and I can really branch out," she says. "No offense, Len. You're fine. It just got so annoying after all these years being in the same room with the same exact set of kids all day long."

"Yeah." I shrug.

We're done with the balloons and I wish there were more because now I don't know what to do with my hands. "Was it weird with them all summer?" I ask.

"I wasn't around that much," Zora answers like I should obviously know this. "We were at my grandma's in Maryland most of the summer. And when I was around, it always felt like they were okay with me being there, but not totally excited."

I put my hands in my pockets and try not to look over at them even though it seems like that's exactly where my eyes want to go.

I didn't expect this—maybe I should have, but I didn't. "What do you think happened?"

"No clue. But I'm over it."

When people say that, it seems like they're actually not but they wish they were.

I walk to the snack table and grab some Tostitos and guacamole, and then I take my plate over to where Sylvie, Annie, and Paloma are standing near the hammock. It feels like there's gum stuck to the bottoms of my sneakers, making it hard to walk. But I have to do it. I have to be over there with them.

"Hey, guys," I say. "Sylv, this guac is sooo good."

"It is, right?" She smiles. "New recipe my mom found online."

Paloma scoffs. "Um, not so new. She shared it with my mom a few weeks ago and she made it for us. We had like eight bowls of guacamole at our sleepover, not even kidding!"

I'm not sure if she's talking to me, or Annie, or both of us.

"I was there." Annie eye-bulges. "Remember? The Avocado Pits. Our band."

They're in a band? None of them even play instruments.

They all start laughing and saying *avocado pits* over and over again and I'm just standing there, trying not to drop my plate. I want to ask Annie and Paloma about their summers. I want them to ask me about mine.

It's like I'm here with them and also a million miles away at the same time.

A few minutes later, Anjali and the art-class girls arrive and I'm over-the-top grateful there are more people at this party, finally. Anjali's the only one of them who goes to school with us. The others went to Hardwick Elementary and will go to Hardwick Middle. Hardwick is the next town over, but it's so close. There's a spot in town where you can literally stand with one foot in Longport and one foot in Hardwick.

"Sorry we're a little late! Also sorry I had to come in my sari!" Anjali laughs at herself. "Honestly not sorry because that's my favorite joke of all."

"Good one, Anj." I smile and suddenly feel an overwhelming need to be close to her. She was never one of my best friends but she was always nice, and sort of side-friends with us. She's goofy and silly and friendly to everyone and honestly, that's the kind of person I need in my life right now, the kind of person I need to be around at this party.

At this party that I HELPED PLAN! I scream in my head.

"How was Indian dance class?" I ask her after a sip of fizzy lemonade. We're on the deck near the table where Sylvie's mom is putting out more food: bowls of chips and Cheetos, a fancy cheese board that you'd see at a fundraiser, more tortilla chips and a few more mini clay pots of guacamole.

"Amazing as always." She smiles and plops herself down on one of the loungers. "Are you going to come to my recital this year? I really hope so."

"Yes, of course." I smile. I think I'd go anywhere anyone

asked me to go right now.

"Lomes, come help me bring out the tray of movie theater popcorn, K?" Sylvie calls to Paloma.

Lomes?

"So glad we're in some of the same classes this year, especially homeroom," Anjali says after dipping a chip into a lump of guacamole on her plate. "Also, yay for honors! We're so smart." She says the last part under her breath. "I did a little dance when the schedules and rosters came in the mail."

"Me too!" I giggle. "Well, not the dance, but I'm so glad, too, I mean."

"It's genius that they just include the rosters with the schedule so no one has to freak out comparing with everyone and seeing who is in what class with them, ya know?" She takes a handful of M&M's out of the bowl and pops a few into her mouth.

"Yeah, for sure." I fill my plate with chips and another scoop of guacamole, and then Anjali and I go to sit on one of the love seats in the corner of the deck.

Even though it feels so nice to talk to her and she's so cheerful and peppy, my eyes keep turning toward Sylvie, Annie, and Paloma, like there's a rope pulling them in that direction. I need to be over there, I need to be with them.

"I am just soooo excited for the sixth-grade overnight," I say when I can't think of anything else. "Sylvie and I have been obsessed with it since we were in third grade, when her sister Ruby went."

Anjali looks at me sideways. "I don't know about this. Tell me more. None of my friends have older siblings—well, except Sylvie, obviously, but we never talked about it."

"So it's this thing where there's like a bonding overnight at this nature-y retreat center for the sixth grade with trust fall exercises and hikes and guided meditation and stuff and it's kind of like a Welcome to Middle School thing but they always do it around Halloween, so you get to wear costumes, and it's basically a Halloween party at night." I get so excited that I start talking really fast. "And they have this partner costume contest with kind of amazing prizes, like fifty dollars to Longport Cones and stuff like that. And literally every year since Ruby went, Sylvie and I have been talking about it and planning our partner costume, like constantly coming up with different ideas. I have a three-page list in my journal."

"Really?" Anjali asks, still chomping on M&M's. "Wow."

"Yeah! I really want to do this soap and loofah costume with her," I explain. "It sounds silly but honestly it looks so cute."

Anjali nods and then looks around the yard, kind of in a wondering-where-everyone-is sort of way. I get a sense that my over-the-topness about the overnight sort of freaked her out.

It starts getting dark, and we all move into the little tents to start the movie. Each one can fit about two to three people so there's a little bit of awkward shuffling.

That's when I regret that I ever suggested this idea.

Sylvie plops herself down in one, and I hustle over but Paloma and Annie squeeze in before I get there. And that's that. No more room. If you had asked me before this party who would have been in Sylvie's tent, I would have said me. Of course, me. No doubt about it.

Callie and the twins from art class stick together like a preschool Popsicle stick creation, so of course they're in a tent together.

I'm with Anjali and Zora and even though I'm friends with them and everything, I still end up feeling like a leftover.

This is not where I'm supposed to be.

My shaky-ground feeling is starting to get shakier, like there's nothing I can grab on to to feel steady again.

I push this all out of my head and try to focus on the movie we're watching—*The Parent Trap*, the one from the 90s, not the original. If I concentrate super hard on every detail and every scene, my worry spiral and soggy-bread feelings won't be able to find their way into my thoughts.

Soon Sylvie's mom and dad hand out the little

containers of movie theater popcorn and we munch on them and watch the movie. Annie's giving a running commentary on Lindsay Lohan, but I can't hear exactly what she's saying, and then every few minutes Paloma cracks up, cackling so loud, it's hard to hear the movie.

I should be having an awesome time at this party. I'm in a beautifully decorated miniature tent in a beautifully decorated backyard and it's not too hot and it's not too cold and I'm eating popcorn and drinking fizzy lemonade. Also, there's cake in my future.

But none of that really matters because my stomach is a smoldering pit of molten lava, reminding me again and again that I'm not where I'm supposed to be.

I should be in that tent with Sylvie right now.

And I don't know what it means that I'm not.

WHEN SYLVIE WAS LITTLE, SHE was obsessed with opening presents at her parties. Then between like second and fourth grades, her mom decided it was kind of mean, and people could tell which ones got all the oohs and aahs and which didn't, and so the opening-gifts-at-a-birthday-party thing ended abruptly.

But apparently it's back now.

The movie is over, and we've had pizza and cake and cupcakes and even chocolate covered pretzels (Sylvie's favorite). It's only eight thirty and pickup isn't until nine, so there's a half hour to open presents.

Anjali and the other art-class girls got her a group gift, so that really speeds up the process. It's a whole set of art supplies—paints and sketch pads and pencils and even a few giant canvases. Her parents got her a fancy easel. Plus her grandma got her a membership to the Met in New York City. She really has all the tools in place to become an amazing artist. Not that she isn't already, but I mean, she's only twelve.

Sylvie opens mine next and my heart pitter-patters with that *Oh, I hope she likes it* prayer circling around and around in my head.

The lady at the store wrapped it so pretty in a shimmery gift bag with rainbow-striped tissue paper; the card is at the top.

"It's a long card, so." I pause and laugh. "You can read it later."

She smiles and nods and puts it to the side with a small stack of other cards. I wonder if she'll really end up reading it. My skin prickles; I've never had that doubt before. She unwraps the tissue paper and pulls out the jean jacket.

"Oh, Len! I love it!" She hops up from the chair and runs over to me and wraps her arms around my neck. My whole body swirls like the foamy milk settling into a latte. "I love it so so so much. Thank you!"

"Yay! You're welcome. I got one too, it has a couple different patches, but it's almost the same and we can be matching sometimes!"

Sylvie nods but doesn't reply, and then she moves on to the next gift.

Zora got her a few tank tops from Look on the Bright Side, one of the classic boutiques in town. Sylvie loves tank tops. She wears them all year long—even in the winter—under sweatshirts and sweaters and stuff.

Of course Paloma and Annie got her a joint gift. I shouldn't be surprised and it shouldn't sting, but it does. Zora wasn't included in that, though, so I guess I don't feel as bad. It's like the matching outfits at this party thing. For some reason all of a sudden, it's Paloma, Annie, and Sylvie attached to one another.

Paloma and Annie got her a whole bag of random stuff: slime that smells like different cereals, bath bombs, lip gloss, another Longport Cones sparkly tote bag with a gift card inside for ten ice cream cones, a personalized glitter phone case and a tie-dye hoodie sweatshirt with rope tassels and pom-poms at the end of them.

"Guys! This is all so amazing." Sylvie sits back in her seat and scrunches her face together like she's choked up and doesn't know what to say. It's unclear if she's talking about the bag from Annie and Paloma or if she's talking about all the gifts.

I think it's all the gifts, though, because she even does a thing where she mentions each one; it's so kind and heartwarming when people appreciate your efforts.

Soon Callie's mom comes to pick her up and Anjali and the art class twins go with them, too. They're all having a sleepover.

My mom comes a few minutes later.

"Do any of you guys need a ride home?" I ask. Paloma lives kind of near me, but truthfully Annie and Zora aren't that far, either. Longport is pretty small and you can get anywhere within ten minutes.

"Oh, um." Paloma plays with a strand of her hair, gazing off into the distance a little and stammering before she responds. "We're actually all sleeping here."

Zora, Annie, Paloma, and Sylvie look at each other. Their faces fall a little, half anxious, half embarrassed.

My cheeks are on fire. It feels like my feet are being pulled into the grass and I'm about to be sucked into a sinkhole at any minute. I scan the backyard as if there's some way for me to disappear, make myself invisible. Is there a word for being the most embarrassed any human has ever been?

My mom and Sylvie's mom are chatting on the other side of the deck right now. My mom is going to literally freak out over this. She's going to do whatever she can think of to fix it and find a way to solve it immediately so that things go back to normal.

And until she fixes it, she's going to be stressed. And miserable. And angry. She's going to scream at me and scream at my dad.

And it's all going to be my fault.

We're standing there, silent, because I guess it's my turn to talk, to reply, to answer them. I don't have anything to say, though. There's no way to respond to this. All I know is that I want to be out of this moment, out of this situation. I don't want to feel this excruciating embarrassment, like I'm the worst person ever, someone whose best friend for life doesn't even want at her birthday sleepover.

"I'm sorry, Len." Sylvie does that scrunched face thing again where the tops of her cheeks touch her eyelashes. "I could only have three people sleep over. You know my mom hates when things get too hyper."

"Um, okay, yeah." I pause, squeezing my eyes tight to force the teardrops to stay back, buried behind my eyeballs. I want to get mad and scream but my voice doesn't come out that way. The words sound meek and wimpy and defeated, even though inside my brain they sound like an animal who breathes venom. "I guess. Um. I guess I'll see you guys at school?"

It comes out like a question even though it's not. Of course I'll see them at school.

"Thanks for coming, Leni," Sylvie says. "And for the tent idea! And the jean jacket."

"Bye, Len," Annie and Paloma say in unison, and then giggle about that.

Zora gives me a look emphasizing all the stuff she was saying earlier. She wants to move on, I get that, but at least she got invited to sleep over! She doesn't even like them and she gets to sleep over!

I feel outside my body right now. Like I'm watching someone else's life. But it's not someone else's life; it's mine. This is happening to *me*. I can't believe it. I can't believe I'm standing here, being forced to accept that they're all sleeping over and I'm not. They'll all be together tonight, having fun, and I'll be in my room, alone.

I pick up the goodie bag on the way out—some gummy ice cream cones from All the Sweets and a set of neon gel pens with a matching set of neon mini marble notebooks.

I don't want any of this. I don't want to remember tonight. I want to run away, sell the house, move to a new town, and then bleach my brain somehow so I can forget everything and everyone. How could this have happened?

I can't believe it. I honestly can't believe it.

"You okay?" my mom asks on the drive home.

What a dumb question. Obviously I'm not okay. And she knows I'm not okay. I'm the opposite of okay. There's not even a word for it. The ickiest, lowest, most horrified, embarrassed that anyone has ever, ever felt.

"Mmm," I mutter, which is not an answer to her question, but hopefully she'll catch on that I'm definitely not okay and that I also do not want to talk about it.

I glance over and see my mom gripping the steering wheel tighter than she was before, her teeth clenched. She's going to make this worse. She's going to make the worst moment of my life even worse than it already is.

I am sinking. My whole entire self is sinking into a deep, narrow hole I'll never find my way out of.

"How could Jill have done this? I've known her for more than a decade!" She fumes. "This is disgusting! She's one of my closest friends! You and Sylvie have been friends since before you were even born!" Her voice is raised slightly but she's not screaming yet. It's more like forceful talking. "We met for tea a few weeks ago, and she didn't even mention it! How could she do this? How could she allow Sylvie to do this?"

I can't respond. I am teeth-clenched, frozen, unable to speak. If panic was a color, bright orange sweat droplets would be pouring out of my skin right now.

She goes on, closer to yelling now. "This is unacceptable. I'm going to call her as soon as we get home. She has to know how completely unkind this was, to leave you out like this."

My mom is going to explode; she's going to start a battle with Jill Bank, Sylvie's mom. I know it. She's going to make this worse. Worse and worse and worse.

"Mom!" I yell. "You can't do that! You can't try to fix everything! You can't solve every problem!"

"Eleni!" she yells. "Don't tell me what to do."

I close my eyes tight and try to pretend none of this is happening.

We get home, and I run up the stairs, not even saying hi to my dad or Pontoon. I kick off my flip-flops and crawl under my quilt, still in my overall shorts.

I toss and turn in bed, shifting my pillow over and up and grabbing one of my shams to put under it. I turn on my ceiling fan and kick my covers off but then I'm freezing, so I grab my sleep sweatshirt and pull it over my head. Then I'm hot again. This goes on for another twenty minutes.

All I want to do is wipe my brain of all these thoughts, like when the little mechanism thing comes down to move the knocked-over pins at a bowling alley. I want to just clear every single part of it away.

"I'm calling Jill right now," I overhear my mom say, all forceful-sounding. I tiptoe out of bed to listen at my bedroom door. I need to stop her. I can't let this happen. "This is not acceptable."

No no no no. She can't do this. Especially not when the other girls are there to overhear.

"Ruthie," my dad says with a groan. "At least let it sit overnight. You're angry, you're upset, rightfully so. But let it sit for now. Things will be clearer in the morning. They always are."

"Jake. This is a line in the sand. Things have shifted," my mom says more quietly, but my ear is on the door so I can still hear what she's saying. "I'm worried."

"I know. I know. But it's going to be okay."

They're quiet then, and I hear the door to their bed-room close. My dad is the voice of reason in this home

38

and I think he convinced my mom to hold off on calling Jill for now. But I don't know what will happen in the
morning.

Suddenly, more than I've ever felt before, I wish wish
wish I had an older sister like Sylvie does. People with
older sisters are the luckiest. They have a bonus person
who's wiser, who's been through stuff and knows how to
help.

Without Sylvie, I don't even know who I am, how I fit
into the group.

And I have no one I can talk to about this. Obviously,
I can't call her. I can't call Maddy. I don't have a sibling;
my mom is out of control. My dad is too busy calming my
mom down.

I am alone. One hundred percent, completely and
totally alone.

AT THREE IN THE MORNING, I pick up my phone from my night table and delete every selfie Sylvie and I have ever taken together—at Longport Cones sharing a banana split, at the beach holding matching pink boogie boards, at Longport Village Pool side by side on lounge chairs, sharing a giant popcorn at the triplex movie theater, standing outside Bizen after we went out for sushi for my eleventh birthday.

There. Done. Deleted.

I get out of bed and walk to my bookshelf. A photo of the two of us side by side at fifth-grade graduation in our fancy dresses. I pull it from the frame, tear it in half and then in half again and again and then finally in a million pieces that land all over my polka-dot rug.

Sylvie! How could you do this to me?

I want to find every photo, every memory, and destroy all of them.

After tiptoeing down the stairs, praying the floorboards don't creak under my feet, I collapse into the oversized armchair by the big window in the den.

My mind keeps going back to Sylvie and Annie and Paloma at the sleepover at Sylvie's. Are they talking about me? Gossiping about stuff that happened over the summer, stuff that I don't even know anything about? I picture them leaning over Sylvie's kitchen island in their socks, eating endless guacamole and chips, and then staying up super late, all eventually falling asleep curled together on Sylvie's gray sectional under a blanket.

And then my thoughts pop over to Anjali's sleepover with the art-class girls. I don't know them as well, but I bet they're having fun. I bet they're laughing about stuff and talking about the start of middle school, sneaking a zillion snacks from the pantry as soon as Callie's parents are asleep.

All I want to do is run away from myself, be somewhere else. I want to get away from these awful thoughts. I need to be out of this moment; I need to stop feeling so heavy.

I shuffle over to the bookshelves in the arched walkway between the den and the kitchen, where we keep the scrapbook photo albums. I take them off the shelves one at a time, about to pull them apart page by page and destroy all the photos of Sylvie and me.

But I can't. Of course I can't. These albums are my mom's passion, her pride, her proof that things are okay, maybe even more than okay. Happy even.

Sitting on the cushioned bench in the bay window with my knees up and the album resting on my thighs, I look through them, one by one, and it's like a real historian documented my whole life. They're proof of something, too, though. Proof that I used to have friends, good friends. Seriously, for real, I did.

Sylvie is my oldest friend, of course. There are photos of us side by side in each other's cribs, on blankets in the park, in baby music classes with the little egg shakers in our mouths.

But early on there was Charlotte too—the first friend that I actually made on my own, in the yellow room at Longport Temple preschool. There we are, holding up the menorahs we made in class—square wooden boards, sloppily painted in various shades of blue, with nuts and bolts glued on to hold the candles in place.

Of course there are lots of photos of Will through the years—my across-the-street neighbor; we moved to Pine Street only a day apart. We're in the bounce house at our annual block party, behind the table at all of our lemonade stands, standing over our bikes with neon helmets strapped to our heads.

I don't know what happened to my friendships with these people. None of them are the way they used to be. I stopped talking to Charlotte when she moved to Oregon, but Will is still across the street, and we're not close anymore either.

My heart is pounding. I should probably put the albums away since looking at them is only making me feel worse, more friendless, like all the good times of my life are in the past and I'll never be happy again, but I can't stop. I need to make it through all of them, to catch up to where we are now. It's like seeing my life in front of me in a slideshow on a giant screen and I can't just stop in the middle.

I make it up to third grade and there's Brenna from Hebrew school—we dressed as twin Queen Esthers for the Purim carnival that year and we were both pieces of parsley in the Passover play. But that friendship evaporated, too.

And then I get to the summer before fourth grade, when I started going to Lake Buel Camp.

Maddy. My first camp friend. My mom kept saying "camp friends are lifelong, the best friends of your life" because of her friendship with Louisa, and I believed her. I really did.

I can't take it anymore. I stop in the middle of the album from fifth grade, last year, from Sylvie's party at the roller-skating place. We're twins in matching hot-pink tank tops and black bicycle shorts and hot-pink roller skates.

I don't know what happened. I don't know how I got to this moment, how all these friendships unraveled. But I need to figure it out. I can't keep going through life failing at friendship again and again. And middle school? Alone? Without Sylvie.

No. I just can't.

My throat tightens up and then it all hits me like I literally walked into a wall.

The sixth-grade overnight next month. Our partner costume. Sylvie as my roommate. All the things we've been waiting for.

All of that is over now. Impossible. Not going to happen.

No no no no no. It can't be. I need to fix this.

My mom needs to not call Sylvie's mom tomorrow and embarrass me even more in front of the other girls. She needs to not freak out. And she needs to definitely not make things harder for me.

Things need to go back to the way they were before the summer.

Half asleep and half enraged, I walk to the front of my house and stare out the dining room window. Across the street, I watch Will's tire swing fly all over the place. It's so windy all of a sudden, and that only makes this night feel even more eerie and lonely and miserable.

I refuse to just sit back and let all of my friendships fade away. I need to do something, take action, and make a plan.

And then it hits me. A mission!

Like with the ear piercing in third grade when we took responsibility for something we really wanted. But obviously this is way more important; there's way more on the line. I mean, I love my pierced ears and we were totally successful and we made it happen, but this is major.

Right here, right now, at four in the morning on September fifth, I declare the start of Eleni Belle Klarstein's Friendship Fact-Finding Mission. I am going to study all of my ended friendships, retrace my steps and figure out what happened, what I did wrong, what I could've done better, and most important, the number one goal of the mission: I am going to get Sylvie back before the overnight. I am going to make her realize I'm her true best friend, her number one, first choice, go-to person. For tent sleepovers and Halloween costumes and birthday-party planning and everything else.

I RUN UP THE STAIRS to my room as quietly as I can, praying that my parents don't wake up. I turn on my desk light and take my journal out of my night table drawer.

Eleni Belle Klarstein's Friendship Fact-Finding Mission starts now!

FriENDships

- Charlotte from preschool
- Will from across the street
- Brenna from Hebrew school
- Maddy from camp
- Sylvie, BFF since the beginning of time

Goals

- Figure out what I did to lose these friends
- Figure out how I can be a better friend
- Figure out what I want in a friend
- Figure out what happened with Maddy and Will and Brenna
- Have an awesome pen-pal friendship with Charlotte & maybe a reunion one day
- #1 GOAL: Be friends with Sylvie again in time for the sixth-grade overnight and have everything be normal and fun and awesome again

Deadline: a week before HALLOWEEN

Why? This overnight has been a thing for Sylvie and me for three years now. I need it to happen. I need it to be great. I need us to be best friends again. I need our costume to be epic. I need all of it to go back to the way it used to be, to be the way it was supposed to be.

After that, I'm sort of stumped. It's the middle of the night and there's not much I can accomplish right this minute. So I do what any sensible journal keeper would do: reread old entries to see what I can uncover.

All my journals from third grade until now.

Brenna IS SO MEAN!!!!!!!!! Right in the middle of the Hanukkah party she told me she's not my friend anymore and she only wants to be friends with TJ and Bette and Jara and then she knocked into me and my whole plate of latkes fell! Applesauce dripped down my leg! I think knocking into me was an accident but STILL SO MEAN!!!!!! SHE IS THE MEANEST PERSON IN THE WORLD. I HATE BRENNA WALSIN!!!!!!!!

The form came from LBC where we get to request who we want to be in our bunk. We always do this thing where I pick Maddy and then she picks Wren and then Wren picks Vivi and Vivi picks Jane and Jane picks Hattie. Everyone is allowed to get one pick and this system basically guarantees that we're all together. Maddy's sister figured it out and it really works. I always worry that one summer they'll change the rules though and try to mix us up. The only one I really care about being with is Maddy even though Wren is so funny and Vivi makes the best bunk decorations and Hattie has the best clothes to borrow. I love them all but obviously Maddy is my number one camp friend.

Halloween was amazing! Sylvie, Paloma, Zora, and I went as mermaids. It was so warm that we didn't even need coats! We did all the streets in the Troutbeck section of the neighborhood where Paloma lives and then all the streets near me and Sylvie. I kinda thought Will would join, but he didn't. He was trick-or-treating with Andrew Culkin and Shai

Remstock and they thought they were so cool because they dressed up as Ninjas.

Sylvie and I were having so much fun at her house after school today. We were doing our favorite thing, spying on Ruby and her friends and then talking about what it'll be like when we go on the sixth-grade overnight. We want to sneak hair dye into our bags and dye our hair in the bathroom, but I don't know if we'll be able to. We want to stay up all night and eat candy and spy on the teachers. But then Paloma called Sylvie and asked if she could stop by because her mom was at a meeting down the street for the school board. And so she said okay. And then she came in and we were still talking about the overnight and then she said, "Leni, you're too obsessed with this; I bet it'll just be a boring school trip." She only said it to me and not to Sylvie. And then Sylvie said, "Yeah, we're just really bored right now." I didn't know what to say after that. I felt so bad that she thought we were having a boring time. Then Sylvie's mom made us cheese fries and we sat in the kitchen and watched this new show on Netflix about a wrestler's family and then I couldn't wait to leave.

I read and read and read until my eyes are so blurry I can barely see the words. I walk to my window just to see if by any chance Will is up too. Maybe his light is on. Maybe he can't sleep. If he's awake, too, maybe I could text him and we could actually talk about stuff.

Maybe he's the first FriENDship to explore.

But no, his light is off, and I picture him cozy and comfy under his plaid quilt. And then I wonder if he still has the blue-and-gray plaid quilt he used to have—I can't remember the last time I was in his room.

I'm sleepy but amped up at the same time and my mind keeps bouncing from Will's plaid quilt to Sylvie's sleepover. And then I feel rage all over again. My feelings need to go somewhere; they need to leave my brain. Maybe once I get them out, I'll be able to sleep.

I take a perfect piece of my personalized Eleni stationery with the neon-yellow Popsicles out of the top drawer and grab one of my favorite thin-tip pens from the cup on top of my desk.

Dear Sylvie,

It's almost five in the morning and you're at your house having a sleepover with Annie and Paloma and Zora and I'm not there and I don't understand why. I helped you plan this party. What did I do that you didn't want me to sleep over? What did I do wrong? Why don't you want to be my friend anymore?

I always thought that no matter what happened to us we'd have each other. I am so confused now and so upset and I don't even know what to do. And all the years since Ruby's sixth-grade trip of us counting down to our Halloween overnight. I can't even picture it now. I can't picture it without you. I can't picture anything without you.

I start crying so hard I have to stop writing.

Okay, I can definitely never send that. Plus starting with Sylvie is clearly not going to work. I grab a tissue and blot my eyes and take some deep breaths. I take another piece of stationery off the pile.

Dear Charlotte,

Hi! Remember me? Eleni Klarstein? Your BFF from preschool? I hope you do.

Well, all is well with me. Kind of. Is sixth grade in the middle or elementary school where you live? For me it's middle and it starts in two days and I'm really, really nervous.

How's life in Oregon? I want to hear all about it.

I'm kind of obsessed with stationery so I was wondering if we could be pen pals and write back and forth.

I hope you're into this idea.

Write back soon.

Love, Eleni

PS Remember how in the yellow room we were obsessed with playing beach? It was kind of funny since we live so close to the beach, so we didn't really need to pretend in class but we did anyway?

PPS Remember the day you brought in pink cupcakes for your birthday?

PPPS okay bye for real now

I address the envelope and put on a LOVE stamp and tuck the letter into my backpack.

I'll mail this to Charlotte tomorrow, and then I'll really be on my way with the mission.

THERE ARE A FEW BLISSFUL seconds right after waking up before I remember what happened last night. But then it ends and everything hits me all at once. My eyes feel swollen and puffy, like they'd prefer to stay closed. They're not ready to face what has happened either.

Outside my door, I hear my parents yapping at each other. Well, my dad is yapping. My mom is yelling.

"I spoke to Jill! And she said that's *always* her rule. No more than three guests for a sleepover or things get out of hand! But can you believe it? Eleni never causes trouble! Jill could make an exception! And Len should be in the top three, of course!" She pauses. I bet she's huffing. I bet her arms are folded across her chest. She's probably pacing in the hallway, scanning her brain for any way to control and fix this mess.

"Okay, let's try to calm down, Ruthie. Deep breaths. Deep breaths," my dad says in his soothing tone. Sometimes I wonder if he does this as much for himself as he does for her. "It's going to be okay. It's one sleepover. I don't think this is going to ruin Leni's life. Let's relax."

"I don't think you understand," my mom says, exasperated already. "In a girl's life, this is a big deal. And Sylvie was her best friend."

Was her best friend? Like it's a known fact to everyone that we're not best friends anymore?

My mom goes on. "And we still don't know what happened at camp this summer! She won't tell us. But she wasn't gushing about camp the way she usually does. She wasn't begging for a sleepover right away with Maddy the way she always does. Mothers can sense this stuff, okay? I need to call the school psychologist! Something's up with Eleni and her friends and it's fair for me to be concerned. I am her mother!"

Suddenly a creepy-crawly ickiness spreads over my skin as more of this horrible reality washes over me. The thing I really, really didn't want to happen, happened. I'm sure Paloma and Annie and Zora are still there, and I'm sure they overheard the entire conversation between my mom and Jill. Worse than that even, they probably think that I asked my mom to get involved, to pick up all the broken pieces. They must think I'm such a baby now, that I need my mom to fix stuff for me.

I don't know how I'll ever show up at school.

The whole year is ruined and it hasn't even started yet.

"She's going to be okay, Ruthie. She's a smart, kind, personable girl. She's resilient. We need to be calm about this," my dad repeats. "We need to show that we're not razzled by it."

"Razzled is not a word, Jake."

"It's not?" He laughs. "Well, it should be!"

I imagine he's putting his hands on her shoulders right now. It's what he does when he tries to calm her down. "It's going to be okay. I promise you."

"Jake, you were never an eleven-year-old girl!"

"I wasn't?" He laughs again.

My mom is probably throwing up her arms now and walking away.

The thing is—who is right here? Maybe they're both right.

I am going to be okay. I have to be okay.

But this is a big deal.

It can be both. Both things can be true.

I crawl back under my covers and drift off to sleep for a little while longer. I have this weird feeling that the longer you stay in bed, the harder it is to get up. It sounds like one of the quirky inspirational quotes Mr. Siskind would have taped to his wall in the guidance office at school.

I step out of my bedroom to pee and brush my teeth and there's no sign of my parents or Pontoon. Maybe they're downstairs in the kitchen or having breakfast on the deck. As I'm leaving the bathroom, I overhear my mom talking in her bedroom.

"Lou, you and Adelaide free today?" My mom talks quietly, but it's loud enough for me to hear her at first, but then it isn't and the words are muted and mumbly. I walk closer to her bedroom door. "I feel pain for her, you know what I mean?" Pause. "Exactly. Like actual, physical pain. You get it."

It's quiet then because I'm sure Louisa is talking on the other end of the phone.

"Sure, a little later would be great." Pause. "Love you too."

I hurry back to my room before my mom can see me, and I flop back on my bed.

My mom is out of control right now. Completely.

First she calls Jill and then she invites Louisa and Adelaide over to intervene.

And I have no idea where to go with this Adelaide visit today. I don't know if I should act excited or be angry or just try and go along with it so I don't stress my mom out even more.

I mean, Adelaide and I have known each other our whole lives because my mom and Louisa have been best friends since they were kids at camp together.

Adelaide and I are snow-tubing-in-the-winter, Coney Island–trips-in-the-summer, apple-picking-in-the-fall friends.

We're family friends. Not friend-friends. A friend friendship is one you make yourself, and even if you don't make it yourself, you cultivate it yourself.

Like Sylvie.

Sure, we met before we were born. But most of the things since—we did them on our own because we genuinely liked each other.

Or at least we used to.

FriENDship: Charlotte
And a little FriENDship: Will

I GET UP, FINALLY, AND throw on my favorite gray pocket dress and my navy hoodie and realize I *definitely* cannot mail the Sylvie letter. But the Charlotte one—that was a good idea. A pen pal is for sure something I need right now.

I head downstairs, hoping I can sneak outside and walk to the mailbox without my parents seeing me and asking a million questions. I know it's Sunday and the mail won't get picked up until tomorrow, but I need to get this letter out of my house. If I wait, I may chicken out. And I need to start this mission. I don't even have two full months until the overnight.

"Hey, Len!" my dad calls out, over-the-top cheerful, from the kitchen, where he's sipping coffee with Mom and reading the newspaper.

"Hi! Just going to mail a letter," I say. "Be back in a minute!" Pontoon runs up to me so I grab his leash from the hook by the door. "Taking Pontoon with me! Bye!"

I hear them muttering and whispering to each other but I ignore it. Can't a girl mail a letter these days without her parents being suspicious?

Everything is still and quiet on the way to the mailbox, but on the way back, Will and Shai are biking in the street, doing that thing where one of them sits on the handlebars yet they still manage to bike around. It's pretty impressive, especially since it's only ten in the morning and they're already hanging out.

"Hey, Eleni," Shai says, really, really unexpectedly friendly, and it catches me off guard.

I think it catches Will off guard too. He sort of looks up at him in this shocked, who-are-you-right-now kind of way.

"Hey," I reply.

"How's it going?" Shai asks.

"Good. Just mailing a letter." I shrug. "And walking my dog." Pontoon pants a little and lies down on the sidewalk.

"You write letters? Like real letters?" Shai asks, sounding like he's just stumbled upon someone from an alternate universe.

"Eleni loves stationery," Will says, almost without realizing it, and then starts fiddling with the spokes on his bike. My heart lights up realizing that he remembers this. It's an actual positive sign for our friendship, for the fact-finding mission, too. "I mean, uh, she said that in class once. So. Uh."

I can't take the weirdness anymore so I interrupt him. "I do love stationery. It's pretty much my favorite thing in the world. I want to open a stationery store one day and call it Len's Pens. But maybe something else more creative. I'm not sure." I pause. "So if you, um, have any ideas for me?" I smile and shrug and settle on the fact that this may be the weirdest conversation I've ever had with anyone, and especially with Will or Shai, and also especially in the middle of our street.

"That's cool," Shai says. "I'll help you think of a name."

"You have time. It's not like I'm going into business tomorrow or anything. Gotta start sixth grade first."

Shai laughs and Will just stands there, still playing with the spokes on the wheels. Pontoon gets up from the ground and puts a paw on my knee and I'm getting the sense that he wants to head home.

"Uh, so, yeah, I better go. I think Pontoon wants water," I blurt out. "See you on the first day of school."

"See ya," Will says.

"Later, Eleni."

I get home from the walk and spend the rest of the

morning out back on the deck, writing in my journal and avoiding my parents.

If I act like I'm fine, my mom will think I'm fine, and then she'll be fine and then she'll meddle less and also not be completely anxious and freaking out.

Sometimes it helps to be a few steps ahead and just pretend things are okay, even when they're not.

I keep waiting for my mom to tell me Louisa and Adelaide are coming over, but she doesn't, and then I start to wonder if I need to act surprised when they show up. This is how eavesdropping gets you into trouble. You know things you shouldn't know and then you need to change your behavior and it's all just super weird.

"Len!" my mom calls to me from inside the kitchen a little while later. "Louisa and Adelaide are on their way over. Want to help me bring out the snack platters?"

"Huh?" I sit up, trying to pretend like I have no idea what she's talking about.

My mom's a great cook and a great baker, but I think what she loves to do most of all is put out a good platter, a fancy cheese board, a good spread, as she likes to call it. She designs them all so artfully, so perfectly, they could be featured in food magazines. And she spends so much time deciding what she'll put on them.

It's probably just another example of her need to control things.

I walk inside and there are platters of bagels and

smoked fish and a beautifully constructed Greek salad with big chunks of feta cheese on the kitchen island. Plus a platter of fruit skewers and a pitcher of lemonade with strawberries floating at the top.

This feels like more of a lunch spread than a snack spread, to be honest. And my stomach is so twisted up there's absolutely no way I'll be able to eat any of it. I hope Lou and Adelaide are hungry.

"You didn't tell me Adelaide and Louisa were coming today," I say finally.

"Oh yeah, just a last-minute, thrown-together kind of a plan," she explains in a rushed kind of way, like she wants me to stop asking questions.

"Um, okay." I plop down on a kitchen chair and Pontoon hops into my lap.

"It'll be fun. They'll be here in a half hour, so please help me bring out some plates and napkins and everything."

I bring the stuff outside and then I take my journal to the hammock. I don't want it to seem like I'm just sitting and waiting for Adelaide to get here.

We're friends and everything since our moms are best friends, but I always feel like Adelaide is cooler than I am, more sophisticated. She's a year older than me and she lives in New York City and part of her hair is always dyed a unique color—last time I saw her, at the end of the school year, it was neon green. She never seems to get fazed by anything and she's super blunt.

I start thinking about Adelaide and me over the years: Are we really true friends if we were sort of forced to be together? I wonder how all this fits into my mission. I start to jot down some notes in my journal.

Categories of Friends

- Family friend (you're friends because your parents are friends)
- School friend
- Camp friend
- Friend from art class / Hebrew school / Gymnastics / Extracurricular
- Group friend (someone you never see one on one, but you're both part of the same group)
- Fringe friend (someone from another group who you're kind of friends with)
- First-choice friend, aka BFF (person you tell everything to, sidekick type)

A few minutes later, I see Louisa and Adelaide coming into the backyard but I don't look up right away. I want it to seem like I'm chill and nonchalant about the visit. I don't want them to know that I know they were sort of forced to come here. I want to give the impression that I'm fine and my mom doesn't need to worry.

I'm realizing that most of all—I really don't want them to feel bad for me.

"Hey, you." Adelaide walks over and plops down on the hammock so hard that it wobbles and I almost tip over the other side. She takes the headphones off my ears and then lies down so we're facing each other. "What's goin' on, LenBurger?"

"Hi!" I sit up and put my headphones and my phone in my pocket. The dyed part of Adelaide's hair is blue right now. It's almost the exact color of her T-shirt.

"How was camp?" she asks me.

"Fine. What about you?"

"Not fine. I was kicked out." She rolls her eyes. I look over at my mom and Adelaide's mom on the deck, to see if they're listening to this, but it doesn't seem like they're paying attention. "It was so lame. A few other girls and I wanted to walk into town to get Chinese food and one of the counselors saw us on the way. So whatever. Kicked out."

"Really?" My heart pounds just thinking about it. Adelaide goes to some fancy all-girls camp where they have to wear uniforms. I've always wondered why Louisa didn't send her to LBC with me, since she went there too, with my mom. "Were you scared?"

"About which part?" She looks at me, a little confused.

"Um, I mean, I guess all of it? The sneaking out and the getting caught and then the whole thing of your parents finding out." I almost wish she hadn't mentioned this to me because just the thought of it feels stressful.

"Not really. Camp is lame. I'm sick of doing all the stuff they force you to do. I mean, when I got home it kind of sucked because I was completely and totally screen free, still kind of am although I need the laptop for summer reading so I sneak onto random sites and email my friends with HELP ME messages."

I laugh. "Oh, wow. This feels like a lot."

"Definitely a lot." She lies back and puts her hands behind her head like a little hammock pillow. "Whatever. You ready for sixth grade?"

"Yeah. I think so."

"It's really no different from any other grade," she says with her eyes closed. "You'll be fine."

Sometimes it feels like Adelaide has learned all the secrets of everything already and other times it feels like she's just trying to pretend that she's wiser and more mature.

"Soooooo." I lift my eyebrows. "What else?" I feel like we've already run out of things to say and it's only been three minutes.

"Nada." She readjusts herself and the hammock wobbles again. "What's this?" She picks up my journal. Pretty sure it's kind of obvious that's what it is.

"Nothing!" I yelp, grabbing it away from her. "I mean, it's not nothing, it's my journal, but please don't read it!"

Adelaide's eyes bulge. "Wow, girl. Calm down."

I put it behind my back on the hammock and wish I'd brought it up to my room before they got here.

"Major secrets in there?" Adelaide giggles. "What's so crazy that I couldn't read it? I mean, I get journals are private but whatevs, we've known each other our entire lives."

This interaction starts to feel annoying and awkward so I blurt, "I know my mom put you up to this, coming here today and everything. You don't need to pretend."

"Huh?" Her face gets all twisty.

"Adelaide."

"Leni."

We both crack up then because this whole thing is so dumb and weird and sometimes you just need to laugh to break up the slimy feelings.

"So what that your mom cares about you and wanted us to come over?" She shrugs. "My mom is lame." Adelaide rolls her eyes toward where my mom and Louisa are sitting on the deck. "Anyway, tell me what happened. Heard there's been drama with your friends. I'm bored. It'll entertain me."

I'm not sure if I should be insulted or not but I let it go. Maybe I should let her read my journal because it may be easier than rehashing the whole thing out loud.

"Want the long version or the short?" I ask, feeling tired before I've even started talking.

"Medium." She shifts into more of a lying down position. "My eyes are closed but I'm listening. Just FYI."

I sigh. "I'm gonna go with the short version. Basically, my best friend since before we were even born didn't invite me to her sleepover party that I helped her plan and then during the pre-sleepover part of the party I realized none of my friends really like me anymore." I pause. It's all really sinking in as I talk.

"So? Find new friends. I mean, it stinks. But they're not the only girls in the world," Adelaide says with her eyes still closed.

"Well." I hesitate. "It's not the first time this has happened," I say so soft it's almost a whisper. My words feel like thumbtacks coming out of my mouth.

Adelaide rolls her lips together and stays quiet for a bit. "That can happen around this age," she muses, like she's so much older than I am. I want to get up and walk away from her ridiculousness. "But it does seem strange and really barfy. I get it."

"Very barfy," I reply, hoping this conversation ends soon.

She stares up at the sky. "So you just write in your journal about it or . . . I mean, does it make you feel better? Maybe you need to talk to a shrink like I do?"

I can tell Adelaide is trying here, but with each second that passes, I want to jump off this hammock and run as far away as humanly possible.

"I guess. I mean, the sleepover thing just happened last night, so I don't really know what'll make me feel better. . . ."

One day I'll get my mom back for this, for calling Jill, for forcing Lou and Adelaide to come over and intervene, for all the things, but in the meantime my mom is already so stressed, I can't make it worse.

I hate the fact that I have to tiptoe around everything because in the back of my mind, I don't want to make my mom's anxiety spiral even more out of control than it already is.

"Writing in my journal does help me sort things out, I guess, and I like rereading old entries, so that always encourages me to keep writing." I sigh.

I go back and forth about if I should tell her about the mission. Part of me wants to, but part of me is feeling kind of embarrassed about the whole thing. I decide to sort of bring it up in a very vague kind of way and see what happens. "But I need to do more than that. I'm going to retrace my steps. My friendship steps."

"Oh, Leni, you're like eleven going on forty." Adelaide cackles. "What do you mean retrace your friendship steps? It sounds like an exercise class at an old-age home."

"Nothing. Never mind," I say with instant regret. I close my eyes and hope we can just sort of stay quiet on the hammock for a while.

A few moments later, I feel a tap on my forehead, and when I open my eyes I see that Adelaide is sitting so close to me that I startle and move backward away from her. "Wow. Too close. Whoa."

"I'm bored," she says, inching back a little, pulling her knees up so they're touching her chin. "I can't just sit here and watch you sleep. I'm sorry I made fun of you; just say what you were going to say."

"Fine." I raise my eyebrows. "Ready? Promise not to laugh?"

"Promise."

"Really promise?"

"Yes. Really. Sheesh."

"Okay." I move back on the hammock a little and hang one leg off the side. "So, after the whole thing with the sleepover last night, I couldn't sleep and I was looking through all the old photo albums and my journals and I realized that I needed to really embark on a mission of figuring out what went wrong with some of my friendships," I say, trying to gauge what Adelaide thinks so far. She's looking off into the distance, communicating with her mom through facial expressions.

"Eleni!" she screams, finally making eye contact with me.

"What?" I reach for my head, figuring there's a giant bug in my hair.

"This is brilliant! You already have a notebook, a million notebooks actually, you've been writing in your journal since you were like six years old, you *looooove* pens, Len's Pens, LOL! It's a no-brainer! Friendship Mission. You were made for this."

I think about it for a moment, suddenly excited. "I was, right? I really was. I mean, not that I'm glad this happened and obviously it's horrible that I've lost all my friends, but the mission. I was made for the mission!"

"Made for the mission," Adelaide repeats. "I'll be your coach, cheer you on, strategize, stuff like that." She nods, all enthusiastic. "At least you have one friend. Me."

I pause a moment, taking all this in. This is kind of the opposite of the Adelaide I've always known—harsh and cold and without much emotion. Also, I'm not sure I really need a coach for this, but I don't want to make her feel bad. I guess it's reassuring that she does consider herself to be my friend.

Adelaide pushes her sunglasses to the top of her head. "Coolcoolcool friendship mission and stuff but also I'm starving and need to eat food. Can we please go grab something from those platters over there? Then we can talk more."

"Yeah, sure," I reply, suddenly suspicious about Adelaide's enthusiasm. Maybe she's mocking me. Or maybe her mom told her to just be supportive and kind, no matter what. Maybe that's what their facial-expression conversation was about.

We walk over to the deck and the platters and spend a while picking at the food and eavesdropping on our moms.

The two of them laugh about things that happened over twenty years ago as if they happened yesterday. They talk about old boyfriends and how it used to take them three weeks to map out a plan to drive on the Long Island Expressway so they could visit each other.

My mom and Louisa are so weird together, almost like they instantly turn into teenagers again whenever they're around each other. I kind of hate it, but I also kind of hope I have a friend like that when I'm old. To be honest, I wish I had a friend like that now.

Seeing them together only makes me feel more alone and friendless. It makes me miss Sylvie and the way things used to be even more than I already do.

"So what's the game plan? Like how do you start something like this?" Adelaide asks as we're walking back to the hammock.

"I wrote one letter," I say, still feeling a little shaky about how much more I should tell her. "And I have a list of the friendships I'm looking into."

"That's good." She hops back onto the hammock.

I scoop the last piece of pineapple out of the plastic cup and pop it in my mouth. "I'm calling it Eleni Klarstein's

Friendship Fact-Finding Mission."

"Say it with confidence!" she demands.

"Eleni Klarstein's Friendship Fact-Finding Mission!" I declare in a whisper-yell so my parents don't hear me.

"K, that's better." She closes her eyes. "I'm tired from all that food. Gonna nap now."

"Um, okay."

A few minutes later, she pops up like a fire alarm just went off in her brain. "What about your old bestie Will from across the street who used to do the lemonade stand with you?" she asks. "I saw him playing tetherball outside when we drove up. Are you still besties? Is he part of the mission, too?"

I'm kind of shocked she remembers Will or the lemonade stands or that she even paid enough attention to know his name.

"No, we're not close anymore at all, actually. Maybe a boy-girl thing." I pause. "He's on the list."

"K." She pulls her part brown, part blue hair into a ponytail and starts fanning her neck. "One thing you need to remember is that all friendships grow and change. I mean, remember my BFF Zoe from my building? We were attached at the hip forever, especially after her mom died, and then she went to a different camp from me and was obsessed with the camp friends and that was that and she barely even talks to anyone at school anymore."

"Oh yeah, I do remember Zoe."

I guess everyone has friendship breakups, and drifting and ups and downs, and times you're closer to the person than other times. I wonder if my mom and Louisa ever drifted apart. I wonder if there will ever be a moment when I feel comfortable asking her that.

"Here's my advice," she starts. "Don't be afraid to just be bold and talk to the people and bring stuff up."

I love how this was my idea and Adelaide mocked it at first and now she's giving me instructions, bossing me around like she's in charge.

"Yeah, okay." I have an all-over shaky feeling, like, will I really be able to do this? Part of me wants her to keep giving me suggestions and the rest of me just wants her to stop talking and forget the whole thing.

"And obviously read through old texts and emails and everything to see if it helps you figure stuff out." She nods, her eyes wide.

"Right, totally." I lean back on the hammock, a wave of exhaustion hitting me. Maybe it was easier, calmer before I brought Adelaide into this. That way if I did it on my own and the whole thing failed, I wouldn't be embarrassed.

"Mmm-hmm," she mutters. "Anything else?"

I sit up straight. "I guess I just feel like all these friendship breakups are somehow my fault. Like what did I do to end up here? And how can I fix it and also make sure it doesn't keep happening?"

Adelaide squeezes her face tight again. "Wow, that

hurts my heart. I need to meditate on this." She pauses. "But first. Show me the list."

I bend down to pick my journal up from the grass, and then I open the page and show it to Adelaide.

FriENDships

- Will from across the street
- Charlotte from preschool—write letters
- Brenna from Hebrew school—maybe piece together old journal entries and texts
- Maddy from camp
- Sylvie. Old BFF.

"I added them in order of when we met, except for Sylvie, since I technically met her before we were even born, and since she's pretty much the reason I launched this mission, I decided to put her last since it'll probably take the most time to figure out." I pause. "I don't know! This is hard!"

"Calm down, LenBurger! Sheesh." Adelaide shakes her head. "You need to chill, light some candles or take a mineral bath or something. Is Pontoon your emotional support animal? Maybe he should be."

Pontoon lifts up his head from under the hammock when she says his name, and we both burst out laughing.

"But do you have any advice for like *how* to do it? Like

I wrote a letter to Charlotte, and I'll try and talk to the others and be bold like you said, but beyond that?" My heart pounds. I feel like I'm putting my entire self on the line right now.

She reaches out her hand. "Give me your journal. I need to write this down."

I hand it to her, along with the pen, and I stare at her as she writes.

FFFM game plans:

- Will from across the street—talk to him face-to-face as often as possible
- Charlotte from preschool—write letters
- Brenna from Hebrew school—maybe piece together old journal entries and texts—chat with her as soon as Hebrew school starts!
- Maddy from camp—reread all the old letters, eventually make a plan to meet and talk?
- Sylvie. Old BFF. Duh.—TBD.

I read along over her shoulder. "*Meet* and talk?"

Adelaide gives me a look. "You'll work up to it."

"If you say so." Seeing it written out like this makes my skin tingle with panic.

She smiles. "Also, Len, you'll figure out a lot as you go." Adelaide's tone has a tint of exasperation. "Not everything in life can be mapped out ahead of time. Take notes and stuff! And don't be so hard on yourself."

"You sound like an inspirational self-help journal." I laugh.

"Yeah, well, maybe that's what you need right now!" She flicks her finger against my forehead.

"Laidey, time to go," Louisa singsongs across the backyard.

"To be continued." Adelaide hops off the hammock and I almost fall.

"Thanks for your help," I say, even though I'm not totally sure I mean that.

"Oh, LenBurger, you'll be fine." Adelaide holds up two fingers in a peace sign.

My mom and I walk them to their car and we all chitchat in the driveway about nothing for a few seconds until they're on their way back to the city and it's just my mom and me standing awkwardly in front of our house.

"I love you, Len," she says. "And I'm here for you. You know I'm your biggest fan."

"I love you, too, and I know that."

I walk around to the backyard, stressing about this Friendship Fact-Finding Mission while already wondering if I'll need another one eventually.

A mission to figure out my mother.

IT'S THE FIRST DAY OF middle school and I can't imagine feeling worse about it. I know that sounds negative and it's not great to feel bad for yourself, but right now I can't help it. Without Sylvie by my side, nothing makes sense. I feel like a naked store mannequin in an abandoned window display.

"Leni, take the jean jacket we got a few weeks ago," my mom calls out to me from the table as I'm grabbing a granola bar. "In case it's chilly in the classrooms. Some are air-conditioned in the middle school."

Is she serious right now? She really doesn't remember that we got Sylvie the exact same one. There's no way I would ever wear that to the first day of school. There's probably no chance I'll ever wear it at all.

"I'll be fine, Mom. It's really hot out."

"Please just listen, Len. You never listen to me," she says, and I can feel her ramping up to start a fight.

"Fine." I take it out of the closet and shove it into my backpack. It's usually easier to just listen to her and do what she says. I definitely don't have it in me to argue right now. My parents tell me three more times to have a good day. I nod and force a smile, and try not to start sobbing. Then I take my water bottle out of the fridge and my backpack off one of the hooks by the front door, and head to the bus.

I look across the street at Will's house and I can't believe it's been two years since I walked to the bus stop with him. Two years since we sat together, every single day, putting our knees up against the seat in front of us, chatting the whole way to school.

And then after school we'd have playdates and I'd be the teacher and he'd be the student. The day my dad brought home the dry erase board and hung it up in the basement for us was honestly one of the happiest days of our whole lives.

Today I'm the first one at the bus stop so I sit down on the curb and eat my granola bar. I want to seem calm and cool, not really fazed by anything. I want to be one of those aloof girls, the kind who makes everyone wonder what they're thinking.

When the bus rolls up, only a few other kids are here waiting with me. I think they're eighth graders because they seem older and are definitely way taller than I am. Even though Sylvie only lives three blocks from me, she's on another route, and I used to hate that, but now I only feel relief.

I get on the bus and it's almost full, so I sit near the front and right before it's about to pull away, I see Will running, his backpack flopping up and down against his back since it's empty.

"Wait," I call out to the driver. "Someone's coming."

Will's breathing super hard when he gets onto the bus, totally out of breath from running all the way from his house. He looks at me for a second and I say, "You can sit here."

Before he answers, he glances toward the back of the bus, and all around, and then he finally sits down on the very edge of the seat, like he's half on and half off, not totally committing to sitting with me but not seeing any other options.

"You almost missed the bus," I say, and then feel silly since it's so obvious.

"Yeah, overslept." He brushes some hair away from his face with the back of his hand and then turns away from me a little, facing the aisle.

I stare out the window, trying as hard as I can to push away these slimy feelings and also tune out the boys in the back who feel the need to scream at each other about a video game the whole ride.

Ten minutes later, I see Longport Middle School. My stomach grumbles in a way it's never grumbled before. I can't believe I'm starting the year mostly friendless. I mean, I have Anjali, sort of, I guess. But she's not a go-to, by-my-side friend. That feels like an essential thing to have at the start of sixth grade, probably an essential thing to have through most of life.

Will gets off the bus a second before I do, and then we kind of walk into school together accidentally. Of course, we didn't plan it this way. He keeps looking around like he's searching for Shai Remstock or one of his other friends. Like it's pretty desperate and he needs to find them right away.

I want him to stay with me, though. Partly for the mission, but also, I don't want to walk in alone. I can't act all excited that he's here with me, and it's true he's said only two words to me this whole time—"Yeah, overslept"—but even still, I want him here.

We walk through the double doors by the gym and there's a lady at a wide table, with her bright red glasses perched on top of her head. She's reading off a clipboard, telling all the sixth graders where their lockers are.

"Hi, Eleni Klarstein," I say.

She looks up at me and then down at her list. "Locker A37. Down the hall, make a left, and you'll see it."

"Okay, thanks."

She smiles. "Have a great year."

"William Spinick," I hear Will say as I walk away from the table. I laugh a little to myself. No one ever calls him William.

I head down the hallway and make a left at the science wing, just like she told me to, and then I see my locker.

And—gulp—I see Sylvie, Zora, Annie, and Paloma, too.

Of all the places for a locker in the whole middle school, of course I have to be right near them. But Longport Middle School isn't like most middle schools, where a bunch of elementary schools join together to make a giant middle school. Longport the town is kinda small and so it doesn't have a huge school district. We have one elementary school, one middle school, one high school. So it's not like we're combining with new kids. It's all of us still together, the way we've always been, just in another building and more mixed up for classes. Of course new kids join every year and some kids move and stuff, but there's only one building for each division.

"Hi," I say to the group, forcing my voice to sound cheery.

"Oh. Eleni. Hey." Paloma smiles like everything is totally fine and normal. She pulls her dark brown waves into a loose ponytail behind her head. Her hair is the lightest I've ever seen it—all these red highlights from the summer sun. She has shampoo-commercial hair.

"Happy first day of school!" Annie sings to the hallway and twirls in a circle. If I could sum her up in one sentence, it's that she's the kind of girl who wears a flowy skirt on the first day when the rest of us are in cutoff jean shorts and she doesn't feel weird about it at all.

The others cheer and Annie twirls again. Sylvie won't make eye contact with me. Every time I look over at her, she looks away. It's like she knows I'm here but doesn't know what to do about it. She flips her head over and pulls her dirty-blond curls into a high ponytail.

I sit down in front of my locker, and Paloma and Annie start grumbling over the summer writing assignment about our names.

"You obviously have the best one, Zora." I smile at her. She knows I'm obsessed with her name.

"Obviously." She smiles a half kind of smile like she's not really feeling it but she's trying.

I have a newish kind of strategy that I just thought of on the bus and I want to try it out a little. Zora is clearly also on the outs with APS, so maybe I can sort of slide into a closer friendship with her. Most of the time we've been group friends, but that doesn't mean we always have to be. We can move into a new category of friendship.

"Did you write about Zora Neale Hurston?" I ask her.

"Of course." She looks at me sideways. "What else would I write about?"

"Well, I mean, yeah. Of course."

Okay, so maybe this sliding into a new category of

friendship with Zora won't be as easy as I had hoped. Seems like she hates me, too.

After that, I stay quiet until the bell rings and I flip through the new notebooks my mom and I got at Eclectics last week. Each one is a different color and on the front they have one word in silver foil lowercase letters: *dream, hope, wish, yearn, passion.*

The bell rings, and I walk down the hall and find Mr. Smith's homeroom, grateful that none of the ZAPS girls are in it with me. I spot my desk; they all have miniature tents on them with our names in thick black letters and on the classroom door it says, "Welcome to the Great Unknown. Happy Exploring!"

Sounds kind of ominous, but I like it. It's a good feeling that teachers are still kind of creative and fun, even in middle school.

I look around, scanning the room for Anjali. A sense of relief washes over me when I spot her. She's in the back with Rumi and Elizabeth and okay, yeah, they're not my best best best friends, but they're the kind of friends I'd sit with if I ran into them at the food court in the mall. We'd push two tables together and all sit and chat and slurp our fountain sodas.

Fringe friends. I'll need to add that to my friendship categories.

The three of them are *best best best* friends, though, so

I'm not sure how I'll fit into that.

I put my stuff down by my desk and walk over to them to say a quick hi before Mr. Smith starts class.

"How were your summers?" I ask Rumi and Elizabeth. I try not to make it obvious that I talked to Anjali at Sylvie's party so I already know about her summer. "It's always such a whirlwind after I get back from camp. I thought I'd see you guys on the beach, but I guess not?"

My mouth is working faster than my brain right now and all these words are coming out and I feel weirder and weirder as I talk. Kind of like the time I got hives from the laundry detergent and at first it started out as one hive and then it sort of exploded so much that eventually my lips were swollen.

"Yeah, we were there, like, every single day of the whole entire summer." Rumi laughs. "I mean, hello, look how tan I am?"

"You always get so tan," I remark.

"I know, and it's weird since my mom is so obsessed with skin protection. Every year when she goes to visit my grandma in Korea she comes back with all these face primers and sunscreens and who knows what." Rumi shakes her head. "She rubs them all over my face like I'm a toddler."

I shift my weight from foot to foot, trying to think of something to say when Mr. Smith bangs a gong, apparently the way he'll call the class to order every day.

I shift back to my seat—between Jasmine Ackerman and Kevin Murray—and look up at the board.

Who are we? Who do we want to be? What do we want to achieve? Let's look back at our past and look forward to the future simultaneously. We can become the best versions of ourselves, the people we were meant to be.

I think about that for a moment and my head starts to spin, sort of in a good way, though. The best version of myself is out there—or I guess in there, like inside me—and I can find it and I can become it.

After homeroom, I have math (with Anjali) and gym (not with Anjali) and then social studies (with Anjali again). And then lunch—ridiculously early, at eleven in the morning.

Anjali and I leave social studies and walk to the cafeteria together and I say, "How do we have every single class together but not gym? I don't get it."

"Oh, because we're in honors everything but for gym, they mix people up," she explains. "My mom told me that's what they said at the intro to middle school thingy in the spring."

"Got it. Okay."

We're quiet the rest of the walk and I wonder what Anjali's thinking about. Maybe she wishes she was with Rumi and Elizabeth right now. Maybe she wishes she had more classes with them. Maybe, like me, she's also completely freaking out about where she'll sit for lunch.

I keep telling myself I'm fine, and lunch will be fine. But more than anything, I wish it was like fifth grade, where we sat at a long table, everyone from the same class together. But I guess even more than that, I wish I just had Sylvie to be with, an automatic, guaranteed by-my-side person.

Anjali walks in a little ahead of me. I bet she's scanning the cafeteria for Rumi and Elizabeth.

Please ask me to sit with you, Anjali, I say over and over again in my head, like maybe she'll be able to read my mind. I feel guilty she's not my first choice but also I'm not sure I can actually sit with Sylvie and them anymore.

I don't know my place. I don't *have* a place.

But I can't sit alone. I *definitely* can't sit alone.

Anjali walks on ahead of me, and she doesn't bring up where she's sitting. I keep walking slowly and then I pass Sylvie's table. Suddenly my feet are frozen in place on this hideous green linoleum cafeteria floor.

Should I sit with Sylvie and them anyway? I mean, I could. There's an empty seat. It would be awkward, sure, but the morning at our lockers was awkward. Lots of things are awkward. It would be better than sitting alone or with people I never talk to. It would be better than roaming the cafeteria, sweat from my hands seeping into the brown paper lunch bag I'm holding.

"Eleni!" I hear someone call out to me from a few tables away.

I look around, not sure who it is.

It's Anjali; she's motioning with her arms. "Come sit with us!"

I hesitate one more second. I wonder if she's calling me over there because she feels bad for me, because she sees me standing here frozen and alone. Or if she really wants me to sit there or if she feels like I can't sit at my usual table after what happened with the sleepover. All of that could be true.

I look at Sylvie and the others one more time.

They're all staring down at their lunches like they don't even know I'm here.

I walk on a little, to the table with Anjali, Rumi, and Elizabeth.

"So glad you're sitting with us now," Elizabeth says when I get there, patting the chair next to her all over the top. "Things change in middle school. It's just how it works. But now that we're all here, we need to discuss something. We need a name for ourselves. Something catchy."

I smile because I can tell she's trying. It feels forced, though, like she really wants to be something she's not, like she's on a path to reinvent herself somehow but needs us to be there along with her.

I'm sitting here today and I'm grateful for that, but I'm not sure it means I'm sitting here every day for the rest of the year. The first day can't seal my lunch fate forever.

I take a bite of my chicken salad sandwich and I try to focus on small things: these girls are nice, my sandwich tastes good, and at least I don't have to worry about the summer math packet anymore.

It's my first middle school lunch and I'm not sitting with my best friend.

FriENDship: Still Will

FOR THE PAST TWO DAYS, Adelaide has been Face-Timing me in the morning. I think it's becoming my alarm clock now.

"Hi," she says. "I'm still asleep."

"You're asleep talking to me?" I ask.

"Yes. I'm that amazing. How's the FFFM?" she asks. "That's what I'm calling it now, by the way. Friendship Fact-Finding Mission is way too long."

I laugh. "Well, it's been, like, two days, so nothing significant has happened yet, and I'm running late and I need to get ready for school." I pause. "Can we talk later?"

"Yes. Bye." She runs her words together.

When I get downstairs, I grab a granola bar and head

to the bus and then my mom stops me. "Len, I can drive you to school from now on," she says. "I switched my schedule a little. Could be good bonding time for us."

I wish she hadn't said the last part. Before that, it seemed kind of nice, but now it seems forced and strained, too much like a project, way too much mom energy so early in the morning.

"Okay, nice, let's start another day," I tell her.

I catch my mom and dad giving each other these looks that say, *I'm worried. What should we do?*

Will's already on the bus when I get there; he's in the back with the boys who scream about video games the whole ride. I try not to feel too deflated that he doesn't want to sit with me again. I'm pretty sure it wasn't his first choice to sit with me yesterday, either, and he just sort of ended up there. But even still, I had a tiny glimmer of hope we'd sit together again and I could make progress with him.

I get to school and unpack everything in my locker. Annie, Paloma, and Sylvie are sitting on the floor in a circle. Zora's with them and not with them at the same time, off to the side just far enough that it's hard to tell if she's part of things or not. Exactly the way it was at Sylvie's party.

Paloma says, "Can we discuss what we're going to do for Halloween costumes? This overnight is such a big deal. I know it's early September, but still."

My stomach sinks.

I'm not included in this conversation, even though I'm sitting right here, and even though Sylvie and I have been talking about this overnight forever and even though Sylvie and I have always done Halloween together. Since kindergarten.

The saddest realization of all is when *always* doesn't count anymore.

I look over at Sylvie but she doesn't acknowledge me at all.

"I have the best idea, guys," Zora says, yelling a little bit. "Little-kid costumes but in a funny ironic way. It'll look sooooo cute. I mean, the whole grade is going to be together. We need to really stand out."

Paloma raises her eyebrows. "Um, that feels weird and no one will really get it, no offense."

"I think we should all go as a rainbow," Annie suggests, twirling a strand of her dark hair around her finger. "It's the easiest, we can all pick a color, and then we can wear whatever we want in that color. It'll look amazing in photos and it's not the hardest thing to pack for the overnight."

"I love that idea," Paloma replies. "Absolute love. And it's so great we're thinking about this now because we need to have it all planned out way before the trip in case we need to ask our moms to buy us stuff. Of course I'm going to be purple."

"Of course," Sylvie adds.

Everyone knows Paloma is obsessed with purple. When her mom let her dye a strand of her hair purple at the end of fourth grade, I swear it was the happiest day of her life.

"We won't have enough colors, though," Sylvie says forcefully. Finally, I feel her looking over at me, but now I can't bring myself to lift my head to meet her eyes.

Paloma considers it for a minute, finishing a bag of pita chips, sort of an odd breakfast but whatever. "So, hmmm. Let's go over this. Maybe it doesn't need to be a complete rainbow." She pauses, thinking about it. "I'll be purple, of course. Sylvie yellow, Annie red. Zora, blue?"

Zora doesn't respond; it's almost like she's not even hearing any of this anymore, or maybe she's pretending not to hear it.

"I really want to be a rainbow, guys, like really, really." Annie huffs.

They're quiet then, sort of staring at each other, and I pretend I haven't heard any of what they've said. I get up and open my locker door and stare into it like all I care about in the entire world is organizing this tiny space even though it's already as neat as it's ever gonna be since school literally just started.

"Let's just talk about this later," Sylvie huffs. "This is annoying and I'm getting a headache. It's so hot in here, and I honestly can't think about Halloween yet. And we only have, like, three more minutes before the first bell."

"I agree," Annie adds. "To all of that."

The first bell rings and Annie, Paloma, and Sylvie scurry off together. Zora hangs back a moment.

"Eleni, are you okay?" She tightens her backpack straps on her shoulders as I bend down to tie my shoelace.

"Yeah. Fine." I choke back the feeling that I'm about to cry.

"Sure? I know it's weird with Halloween and the overnight and Sylvie's party. I mean, everything is weird with them. I still want you to be included."

"Oh, um, thanks." I sniffle.

"I still feel really bad about the sleepover," she starts as we walk together to our homerooms. "All summer, it kind of felt like the three of them only wanted to be with each other. And Paloma went to Spain to see her family for a week but that didn't seem to change things between them. They texted literally all day long, even with the time difference." She pauses, sort of like she's waiting for me to respond. "I don't know."

"Yeah. I'm not really sure what's happening," I stammer. I didn't expect this conversation to take place and I'm sort of surprised by how hard it is to talk about.

"Well, anyway, just wanted you to know I felt bad."

"K, um, thanks, I guess." I stop because I'm about to turn and part ways with Zora to head to my homeroom. "See you later."

She nods. "See ya."

I get to the classroom and Rumi and Elizabeth walk in a minute later. They stop at my desk. "Eleni, you can sit with us every day at lunch if you want. Not sure if it was, like, a first-day thing." Rumi scratches her cheek. "It can be permanent. Just wanted you to know."

"Um, okay. Thanks." I smile. It seems like she's continuing a conversation I didn't know we started.

"Because, like, the whole thing at Sylvie's," Elizabeth adds. "We weren't invited, obvs, but we heard about it and we felt really bad."

"Oh my goodness!" I yell, and clamp my hand over my mouth because I really didn't mean for it to come out so loud. It's so early in the morning and every conversation is off-the-charts intense so far! "You guys don't need to feel really bad! No one needs to feel bad! I'm fine. Look at me." I stand up and twirl around in my *Beach Vibes* tee with my jean shorts. Truthfully, I don't know why I twirl. It just sort of happens. "Don't I look fine?"

They giggle. Under her breath, Rumi says, "Um, Eleni. What are you doing right now?"

My cheeks catch fire. "I don't know," I whisper, and sit back down.

"K, well, um, see you in a bit, I guess," Elizabeth says.

Mr. Smith starts class and the same prompts are on the whiteboard even though we don't have to answer them every day.

Who are we? Who do we want to be? What do we want to achieve? Let's look back and look forward to the future simultaneously. We can become the best versions of ourselves, the people we were meant to be.

I definitely don't want to be the kind of person that others feel bad for.

FriENDship: Will. Again.

AFTER SCHOOL, I GET OFF the bus and Will is playing tetherball in his front lawn.

"Will, you're home already?" I say, shocked. I've been planning to dive in, really launch this part of the mission, and was just waiting for the right moment. Last time he was with Shai and I was just starting to figure things out. I was hoping for a day when I'd see him outside so we could really start talking and that day is here! "Did you go to school today?"

He looks at me crooked, like he's out of practice talking to me. "I left early." He keeps playing and doesn't really make eye contact.

"Everything okay?" I ask.

"Uh. Yeah." He still doesn't look at me; he seems really confused that I'm talking to him right now.

"I'm gonna go grab a snack," I tell him. "Want one?"

He hits the ball one more time, super forcefully, and then lets it swing around the pole a few times. Finally, he looks up at me. "Does your mom still buy those fruit punch pouch things?"

My cheeks prickle like I'm getting somewhere with this, a tiny step in the right direction. "Sometimes!" I reply, sounding way too excited for a conversation about fruit punch pouches. "Let me go check if we have any."

"Cool, thanks," he mumbles.

I walk inside and drop my backpack and my dad calls out hello from his upstairs office. He's a contractor, so he has to visit multiple job sites every single day, making sure everything's going well. In the afternoon, he tries to do all his paperwork and calls and stuff so he can be home when I get back from school.

I scan the pantry for the fruit punch pouches like finding them is the most important thing I've ever done in my whole entire life.

As I search, I think about our friendship. It feels like it was a "one day we're friends" kind of thing, and then "one day we just aren't friends anymore."

A complete before and after, but there wasn't a thing that divided it.

And so much of our friendship was about proximity,

closeness, the fact that our parents chose to buy homes on Pine Street. I mean, if one set of parents had decided to live somewhere else, our friendship would never have existed.

"Dad!" I scream upstairs, hoping he'll hear me, while I take every single item out of the pantry. "Dad!"

"Coming!" I hear his feet padding down the stairs. Out of breath, he says, "What's going on? Everything okay?"

I laugh for a second, but then I feel bad that he thought this was an emergency. "Just wondering if you know if we have any of those fruit punch pouches," I say.

He shakes his head. "This is what you were screaming about?" He walks toward the pantry and takes a quick look in. "I don't know for sure; keep looking. Back to work for me!"

Pontoon lies down by my feet.

"Tune-Tune, what do you think?" I ask, rubbing his head.

He looks up like he's trying to search, too.

Finally, I find two smooshed-in pouches behind a metal box of decaf English Breakfast tea and a bag of rotini pasta.

I grab them and run back outside.

Of course Will isn't out there anymore. I guess he gave up since it took me a while to find the pouches.

I sit down on the porch and start to jot down some

thoughts on the notes app on my phone. I'll copy them into my journal later.

> **Things about Will and my friendship with him:**
> - We moved to Pine Street one day apart
> - He has a much older twin brother and sister so it was always kind of like he was an only child too
> - We used to have a lemonade stand together every year
> - We'd race on our bikes around the block and especially on Mr. & Mrs. Malm's circular driveway
> - We used to sit together on the bus
> - We barely say hi to each other anymore
> - Our moms aren't friends
> - Our dads chat from time to time
> - What changed?
> - Do I miss Will as a friend?
> - Was it my fault we drifted and can I reset the drifting?
> - Can boys and girls even really be friends once they're in middle school?

I wait a little while longer for him to come out again, and then I give up.

I go inside and look through my old journals again to see if I missed any entries about Will. I find another one from last year.

The weirdest thing happened today. We had a half day because of fifth-grade teacher development day and also Earth Day and all the fifth graders were supposed to go home and pick up trash around their neighborhood. I picked up five pieces and then I was done so I was in the front yard throwing sticks to Pontoon and then Shai Remstock and Will came over and started playing with Pontoon too. I hadn't talked to Will in so long and it felt so weird to hang out with boys but then it was actually kind of fun and Shai said he loves dogs and I think Pontoon liked them too.

Maybe I can't just wait until I see him outside; I might need to be bold, like Adelaide said, ring his doorbell or something.

But I feel like I'm at least making progress with my mission; I'm on a path.

One friend at a time, I guess.

FriENDship: Charlotte!

THE NEXT MORNING, I COME downstairs to grab my granola bar and head to the bus and there's a letter waiting for me on the kitchen table.

It's from Charlotte!

My dad looks up from the paper. "Oh yeah, this came for you." He smiles.

I'm surprised I have a reply from Charlotte so soon and that mail is so speedy! This has to be a good sign for the mission. I open the letter and my dad stares at me like he's waiting for me to explain why I suddenly have a pen pal.

"I decided to finally put my stationery to use," I explain. "Like for real, actual letter writing."

"Good idea, Len." He smiles.

I'm overwhelmed with relief in this moment that my mom is already at work. If she were here, she'd ask me a zillion questions about this letter, why I wrote it, what Charlotte said, if we're going to keep writing. Either my dad doesn't care or he doesn't know what to ask, but either way, this moment is just for me and this letter and I like it that way.

Dear Eleni,

It's so good to hear from you. I think about you sometimes and wonder if you still remember me. Of course I remember you! I remember all the things you mentioned—playing beach ALL the time and the cupcakes. I don't live near the beach anymore and I really, really, really miss it. My mom really loves living near my grandparents though (her parents) and I like that part of it, too. We see them almost every day. They live down the block.

School feels kind of the same for me this year, no real drama, except my best friend, Nina, moved to Atlanta at the end of last year so it's kinda lonely without her.

We were backyard neighbors and when I look in my backyard and I don't see her, I get really sad and wish she was still there. But other than that, things are kind of okay with my friends. Tell me about what's going on there and why things are weird.

Oregon is cool. It's very relaxed and low-key and the people are nice. I don't really know. It's kind of hard for me to remember Longport now. It's like a foggy memory.

We can definitely be pen pals.

Does that girl Sylvie still live near you? I remember she had the most amazing toys. She had like six of those Bitty Babies! Hahaha random.

Write back soon.

Love, Charlotte

I read her letter over three times and it feels soothing like a bowl of miso soup from Bizen on the coldest possible day. Just knowing that someone from a really long time ago actually remembers you—it makes you feel good, like you matter.

It actually fires me up; it's an undeniable sign of progress.

I tuck the letter in the front pocket of my backpack because just having it there will add a much-needed layer of confidence to my life. I say goodbye to my dad and grab my daily granola bar and head to the bus.

When I get to homeroom, Anjali, Rumi, and Elizabeth are already there, chatting in the back near Mr. Smith's little library.

"How's it going, Eleni?" Rumi asks. She always uses my full name and it's kind of startling. It's like she doesn't feel close enough to me to use my nickname.

"Fine, good." I laugh. "The usual. You?"

"Good," Elizabeth answers for both of them. "Did you hear what's happening today?" She's kind of like the reporter and organizer of the group, I'm realizing. She likes to update us on stuff, think of group names, sort of oversee stuff.

"No," I reply. "I don't think so."

Rumi pats her knees while standing up, trying to do a drum roll. "At assembly today we're going to hear more about the overnight! You were telling Anjali about it at the party we weren't invited to, right?" She scrunches up her face into a goofy kind of smile. "Just kidding. I mean, not kidding about telling Anjali, but about the party thing."

"Okay, stop with that already!" Anjali rolls her eyes. "Also, woo to the overnight!" She cheers and half the class turns around to see what's happening.

"Wait, today?" My stomach sinks. I don't think I'm ready for this.

"Yup! I thought you were so excited for it?" Anjali asks me, scratching an itch on her forehead.

"Yes, um, definitely."

"You don't seem so excited right now," Rumi says, confused, basically just blurting out whatever she's thinking. "Anyway, it really sounds so awesome."

"For sure," Elizabeth adds. "My neighbor told me at the end they have a friendship circle and everyone goes around and says, like, a new thing they learned and appreciate about a person."

I want to say how stressful that sounds, and how awkward, and how awful I'll feel if no one says anything about me. But I don't. I just smile and nod and try to act like everything is great.

As nice as Anjali, Elizabeth, and Rumi are, when I'm with them, I get this sense that I'm playing some kind of part. Like I'm not myself. I don't fit with them but at the same time it's not the worst. It's this neutral, bland-gravy kind of feeling that I instantly want to run away from, but then I realize I have nowhere to run to.

Mr. Smith comes in a minute later and does his whole gong routine. He's also started us on this morning meditation where we sit quietly for three minutes and try to focus on our goals for the day, our goals for the week, and our goals for the month.

He turns to the board and writes our daily *Ponder This Prompt*.

Think about your first memory. What is it? Describe with as many details as you can. Now ask yourself this: Is this a memory you recall from when it actually happened? Or is this a memory you recall from a photo? Take your time! Don't rush! Put all pieces on my desk when you're finished.

I sit there and tap my pencil eraser against my notebook. My first memory. Hmm. I think back to my birthday parties. I don't remember my first even though I've seen the pictures with chocolate cake smeared all over my face. I think back to my second and even that's a little fuzzy.

And then I remember—baby music class—when I was two and a half. My mom and I went every week and we sat on the red rug in the karate studio and there was this one xylophone that I was obsessed with and I would try as hard as I could to get it before any of the other kids did.

Sylvie was in the class, too. Of course she was. Our moms did everything together back then. I wonder if she remembers. I heard Mrs. Tolin's homeroom doesn't do these writing prompts; it's a Mr. Smith thing. So maybe she's not on a walk down memory lane like I am right now.

I spend all morning worrying about the assembly. Finally the bell rings at the end of social studies, and Anjali and I walk to the auditorium together. My stomach gurgles with nervousness and hunger and it's hard for me to even follow our conversation.

The grade shuffles in and I sit quietly in my seat, my whole body feeling pinched and unsettled. Ms. Baldour, our principal, starts talking and it's mostly about adjusting to middle school and combination locks and switching classes and how we're going to start having more tests. But then she says, "We know you've all heard about the famous Longport Middle School sixth-grade overnight, and we're trying something new this year!" My heart sinks with the overwhelming feeling that things are going to get even worse. "To get the students more involved in the planning."

If none of the sleepover stuff had happened, Sylvie and I would be reaching over to each other right now, down the row, touching hands and scrunching our faces together in silent excitement. But I can't even look in her direction. She's across the auditorium from me and I make sure my gaze doesn't ever wander anywhere close to her.

"Friday after school, come to the gym if you want to join the overnight planning committee. No pressure, but the more the merrier." She smiles and dismisses us and tells us not to dillydally in the hallway and go straight to our next class.

"Yeah, it is going to be so, so epic," I hear Sylvie telling Paloma as they leave the auditorium. "Ruby said she and her friends stayed up all night and the teachers didn't care. And the retreat center where they have the overnight has this coffee machine and they even let the kids use it to make all these French vanilla and hazelnut coffees."

"I am sooooooo excited," Paloma says, picking up her

backpack and throwing it over one shoulder. "Like this may be the best night of our whole lives."

I watch the two of them walk down the hall together, arms linked, and it feels like an imaginary force is poking toothpicks into my skin.

The way they talk about the overnight, making it sound like it was *their* thing all along. It's like Sylvie forgot about all of our plans or she forced them out of her brain; she threw them out the car window of her mind and they landed on the sidewalk. Paloma hypnotized her or something when they were at the beach this summer. I don't know what happened, but it can't stay like this.

I want to join this committee; I want to be part of the planning, even if I do it on my own. But if Sylvie joins, too—I can't imagine that. I can't even picture what that would look like, how I would face her, how it would feel to be in a room together.

Just the thought of it makes me want to switch schools or maybe just crawl under my covers forever.

I get home from school and my dad's in his home office on phone calls and in video meetings with clients.

Pontoon follows me out to the front porch and I sit on the wicker rocking chair, waiting to see if Will comes home. It's almost five o'clock, he's gotta be home sometime soon.

"Hey, Len Len." My dad comes out and sits next to me on the other wicker rocking chair. "How was school?"

"Fine!" I chirp. "Nothing crazy."

"Okay," my dad replies.

I nod and sit back in the chair. "Yeah. Not much new, really."

I look across the street. Still no sign of Will.

"Things are okay with your friends? Sylvie and Zora and everyone?" he asks quietly, and I know he knows Annie's name and Paloma's too, but he tries to keep it chill, nonchalant, like we're just having an easy-breezy little chat.

"They're fine," I answer. "Don't worry."

He giggles. "I'm not worried, Len. Okay, of course I'm worried! It's our job to worry."

I glare at him. "We both know Mom's the worrier in the family."

"True." He smiles. "But I worry too. Of course I do."

"Of course you do."

We both start laughing and it seems like my dad accomplished what he set out to with this little chat—just letting me know he's aware of what's up and he's here for me. And I obviously already knew that, but it's still good to be reminded of it at times.

"All right, back to work for me." He pats his thighs and gets up. "This project is taking over my life."

I stay outside on the porch, realizing I should probably go in and do homework, but I don't feel like it just yet. I decide to text Adelaide.

Me: Heyyyy

Adelaide: Hey

Me: What's up?

Adelaide: Nada u

Me: Not much

Me: They're having a student planning committee for the overnight

Me: I want to join but I'm scared

Adelaide: DEFINITELY JOIN

Adelaide: You and Sylvie can work together and you can get this mission solved ASAP

Me: You think?

Adelaide: YES

Me: Ok

Me: Actually will is coming out rn

Adelaide: Go go. Crush this thing.

Will comes outside a few minutes later and I wonder if he's been home this whole time or if I somehow missed his mom pulling into the driveway. He sits down on one of his front steps, eating a bag of microwave popcorn. It's hot so he jostles it from hand to hand and it makes me laugh.

I get up from the rocking chair and Pontoon looks up at me, probably wondering if he should come along or not. I think yes. Dogs break all tension. Dogs make everything better. Plus he's already my assistant, partner in crime of life and this mission, so duh. Of course he has to come.

"Let's go, Tunes." I grab his leash and we walk across the street, my heart pounding—hopeful and excited.

FriEndship: Still Will

"HEY, WILL," I SAY, STANDING at the edge of his lawn. "How's it going?"

He peers deep into the bag of popcorn and pours some into his mouth. Must have been a few kernels in there because his crunching is really loud.

"Oh." He looks up at me. "Hey."

"How's it going?" I walk closer to the steps. Pontoon follows and then he lies down in a patch of afternoon sun.

Will stares into the bag again and picks out one stray piece of popcorn and then puts the bag down. "Nothing. Uh, I mean, fine."

I laugh. "Can I sit for a second?"

"Uh. Yeah, I guess?"

So far it seems that William A. Spinick has no recollection of our friendship or even me as a living human person.

"So what's new?" I ask him, sitting down on the way other side of the step, pulling at a dangling thread from my jean shorts pocket.

"Huh?" He looks at me like I'm speaking another language.

"What's new?" I say. "How's math this year? You have Mr. Palacco, right?"

"Yup."

"Sooo." I stretch out my legs and try to appear all casual even though this conversation feels like someone is pulling my teeth out with tweezers. "How do you feel about the overnight coming up?"

"Um, haven't really thought about it." He stares up at the sky for a few seconds and then looks back at me, squinting. "Eleni, are you okay? Do you need help with something? Or, like, what's up?"

"I'm fine!" I giggle; I hate that I do that so often when I'm nervous. "We just haven't talked in forever, and I saw you outside so I figured I'd come and say hey and see how sixth grade was going for you. And I brought you a fruit punch pouch! I added them to our ongoing grocery list!"

He looks up and I throw it to him and he catches it in a clumsy kind of way.

"Oh. Wow. Thanks. Yeah." He finally smiles a little,

more of a sideways, confused smile, but it's something. "Sixth grade is going good, I guess."

"Yeah, well, that's good." I try not to look at him like something's not quite right, even though that's exactly how I feel.

"What about you?" he asks.

Finally! A chance for me to talk about stuff and maybe pull him into an actual conversation.

"It's going pretty well for me," I start. "Mr. Smith is an awesome homeroom teacher, not excited about the tests thing though, and yeah." I pause, hoping he'll reply to one of the things I said.

"Cool, well, uh, I better get inside and start homework." Will stands up. "I had an orthodontist appointment after school, so, um."

"Okay." I stand up, too. "Maybe we can hang out another day? Or, um, chat or play tetherball. I like tetherball! Reminds me of camp!"

I feel myself coming on too strong with this. But I can't seem to stop.

"Uh, yeah." Will nods again. "See ya, Leni."

He walks back inside and I'm left on his front porch, standing there like some kind of lazy intruder. On the bright side, he called me Leni. My nickname.

Like he still knows me.

An absolute sign that there's hope for us.

FriENDship: More Charlotte

AFTER DINNER, I GO UP to my room and check my phone and notice that I have six texts from Anjali.

> **Anjali:** Hiiiiiiiii
> **Anjali:** Eleni!
> **Anjali:** Where are you?
> **Anjali:** Answer meeeeeee
> **Anjali:** Do I have the right number?
> **Anjali:** Eleni where are youuuuuuuu

I text back right away.

Me: Hiiiiii. I was having dinner. Chicken fajitas. Yum

Anjali: Yummmmmmmmmm

Anjali: Actually can I call you?

A second later the phone rings and Anjali says, "Hi. So sorry. I know it's weird to call right after texting but my fingers couldn't type anymore and it was too much to text anyway."

"Oh. It's okay." I look out my bedroom window to see if Will is outside again. He isn't. "What's up?"

I start to feel twitchy about this call, worried about awkward silence and lulls in the conversation. Anjali and I aren't phone friends yet. We're barely text friends.

"Sooo," she starts. "I was talking to Sylvie after art class and she said that she heard from someone, I don't know who, maybe a teacher, that the rooming situation for the overnight is actually three to a room now. There are like a few two-person rooms but the whole building at the retreat center where we stay got redone and now it's mostly three."

"Oh. Um," I reply. I don't remember discussing the rooming situation with Anjali, so I don't really know why she's telling me this, and they didn't mention it at the assembly so I have no idea how Sylvie knows this in the first place.

"Yeah, so, like, I just wanted to tell you," she says, and I'm too nervous to ask any more questions.

"Oh, okay, um, yeah, I remember when Ruby, Sylvie's sister, went it was all two to a room," I add, for no real reason. It feels like when someone brings up a movie that came out a million years ago and no one cares or even remembers it anymore.

"Yeah, I guess it changed. Anyway, I didn't want you to be caught off guard." She pauses. Here's the lull, the silence. I pick at a patch of dry skin on my scalp, praying for words to fill this empty space. "But anyway, Elizabeth and Rumi are really happy you're sitting at our table for lunch now."

"Oh, nice." I pause. "Yeah, I'm happy too."

I lie. I totally lie. I'm not happy. I'm the opposite of happy. They're nice and everything, but they're not my friends; they're not my people. Their table is not where I'm supposed to be.

"Are you going to the overnight planning meeting?" Anjali asks me. "I really want to but I have Indian dance and my mom won't let me skip."

I swallow hard, suddenly realizing I'll probably be sitting alone at this meeting. "Yeah, I think I'm gonna go." I pause. "But, um, I need to finish homework now, Anj," I say. "So, yeah, um, see you in school tomorrow."

"K, I do, too. Bye, Leni."

I sit at my desk, frozen for a minute, realizing what this means. Three to a room is the worst possible setup. That means Annie, Paloma, and Sylvie will be together and

Rumi, Elizabeth, and Anjali will be together. Who knows about Zora but all she wants to do is find new friends anyway. Plus even if she did room with me, we'd need another person and then we'd just be a lopsided, uneven group of people who don't really want to room together in the first place.

I need to fix this right away. Before my mom finds out that I have no one to room with and she calls the school and demands that parents come to chaperone, so she can be my roommate. I need to fix this before my mom calls Jill Bank sobbing, begging for Sylvie to be with me and I feel the most pathetic.

I sit there, staring out the window, trying to stay calm.

I take my stationery box out from the bottom shelf in my closet and pull out my fanciest set. It's eyelet trimmed with little gold pineapples embossed on the top, and each envelope has a gold lining and then one tiny pineapple on the back flap.

Stationery is literal calm to me. So neatly organized and arranged, and each piece is unique and beautiful in its own way.

Len's Pens. It's going to be the most perfect store in the world.

Dear Sylvie,

What did I do wrong? Just tell me. How could you just forget all about me like this? Out of nowhere. We were best

118

friends. Literal best friends. You said it yourself a million times. You said I was more like a sister than Ruby even. Please just tell me what I did. I want to fix it. I want to make it better. It's probably all my fault. But I need to know what I did so I can fix it. I can't go through life without you by my side.

Eleni

Okay. I'm not sending that one either. But it's still good to get my rage out in letter form. Time to write back to Charlotte.

Dear Charlotte,

SO happy you remember me and how much fun we had playing beach. That's sad about your backyard neighbor moving away. I'm in this crazy friend drama with Sylvie actually. She just randomly, like, stopped being my best friend. Did that ever happen to you with someone? She didn't invite me to her sleepover and now we don't talk and we have this school overnight coming up around Halloween and I don't know who I am going to room with.

Ugh. Sorry to make this a whole letter of complaining.

Write back and tell me what's new at your school.

XOXO Eleni

15

ON FRIDAY WE'RE AT OUR lockers after school and my stomach has been a Ferris wheel all day, waiting for this planning meeting. I quickly take out my phone to remind my mom I'm staying after school and I see I have a few texts from Adelaide.

> **Adelaide:** Good luck with the meeting
> **Adelaide:** Shoot eye daggers at Sylvie
> **Me:** OMG WOW STOP
> **Adelaide:** Calm down I'm kidding

I'm going to the meeting alone because Anjali is busy with Indian dance and art class right after and Rumi and Elizabeth just didn't seem so interested.

"I'm fine with whatever this overnight is," Rumi said earlier. "I don't need to plan it."

She didn't mean to say it rudely, but the words sort of tumbled out of her mouth that way. I think that's just kind of how she is at times.

"Honestly. I'll go to this one meeting but I don't really want to spend forever on this," I overhear Paloma say to Sylvie and Annie, closing her locker so hard it's almost like a slam. "We have so much work to do and my mom is forcing me to get a tutor for math already."

"It won't be that bad, Lomes," Sylvie says under her breath. "Calm down. They said it'll be really short; I'll have plenty of time to get to art class."

Annie adds, "I'm only going because my mom really wants me to get more involved with school stuff. But I guess it does seem kind of fun."

Zora flips her head over and pulls her braids into a ponytail. "You guys tell me how it is and maybe I'll go to the next one. My mom doesn't want me skipping gymnastics."

I pretend I'm not listening to any of this, but it's not necessary because none of them even look over my way. I'm invisible.

Somehow it feels like going to this meeting is the last thing in the world I want to do and the most important thing in the world for me to do at the exact same time.

I wait for them to start heading to the gym and I hang

back a little. It feels easier to walk into this meeting right when it starts, not have any of that pre-meeting chitchat. I need to be all business about this. I need to act like I have it under control.

As soon as Paloma, Annie, and Sylvie turn down the science wing, I start walking over there.

My heart pounds in rhythm with my steps somehow and I try to do some deep breathing to calm myself down.

It's fine. It's one meeting. I'll get there right as Ms. Baldour starts talking and quickly duck my head like I'm sorry for being almost late and then sit down. No small talk or chitchat or awkwardness at all.

I'm almost at the gym when I hear Will's and Shai's voices behind me. I keep walking, pretending I don't know they're there.

"Oh, hey, Eleni," Shai says when they catch up to me, like he almost didn't expect to see me here, but it is a hallway at our school so I don't know why it's so surprising.

"Hey, you guys going to the meeting?" I ask, my voice catching in my throat a little at the end, like I haven't said words in a while.

"I am," Will says. "Shai has cross-country."

My heart swells a million inches at that moment. I don't need to walk into this meeting alone! I was fine to do it, but now I don't need to!

"See ya," Shai says, turning to head into the locker room.

"So, what's this all about?" Will asks me.

"Um, a planning meeting for the overnight?" I'm confused by his confusion.

"Oh yeah, well, like, do we get community service credit for this?" He looks at me, and genuinely seems so baffled. I wonder how he landed on the idea to go to this. "That's why I'm going."

"Maybe?" I shrug.

We walk into the gym and everyone's already seated around this big, long table with Ms. Baldour at the head of it.

"Come in, guys, we're about to start," she says. "Welcome, everyone, to the planning committee for the sixth-grade overnight! We're so excited you're here."

I look around the table and it's a pretty big group of people. Sylvie, Annie, Paloma, me, Will, Abe Melman, the triplets who live around the corner from Zora, the new girl who's in gym with me, and a bunch of other random kids I've been in school with forever but I don't really know so well.

"This won't be a long meeting; I know a lot of you have extracurriculars on Fridays. And this committee won't really be too much work, so don't worry," she says. "We just want to have an open dialogue about what this overnight means, how we can make it as meaningful and impactful as possible." She smiles and looks out at the table. "First of all, we've had some parents who suggested the Halloween party component actually happen at school the night before the trip, so they can see their kids in costumes and take pictures. Plus we've had many costumes mishaps over the years, and upset sixth graders. . . . Sooo, what do you all think of that?"

A feeling of relief washes over me. Maybe this is the best possible thing. That way if the party is a nightmare, I can go home and be alone in my room and not have to face a roommate and pretend everything is fine. I want to say *yes, definitely,* but I can't be the first to speak up. I don't want to be the first to speak up.

"That sounds cool to me," Abe Melman says, not overly enthusiastic-sounding but excited enough to answer right away.

"Me too," one of the triplets answers. "My mom is a makeup artist and it would be such a bummer if she can't help us with our costume makeup."

"Ooh, good point," Annie chimes in. "Yeah, this is a very good plan."

"I agree," I add; my words come out quieter than I'd like them to.

I feel Sylvie looking at me but I don't make eye contact with her. Being so close to her makes me feel a little uneasy but also empowered—like I don't have to look back at her and see her facial expression right now. I can just sit here and do my thing and pretend not to worry about what she thinks of me.

"Any objections to this?" Ms. Baldour asks. "Speak up. All opinions are valid."

It's quiet; everyone is looking around the table at each other.

"Okay, perfect," Ms. Baldour says. "Seems we're all in agreement. That's really all I wanted to discuss as a large group today. I'm going to pass around a clipboard with a sign-up sheet. Please put your name and email on it and I'm going to divide you all up into groups of three. At the next meeting, you'll brainstorm ideas for meaningful, fun activities for the overnight and then submit them to me and I'll go over them with the faculty. Plan on another short meeting next Friday." She folds her hands on the table. "Thank you all so much for coming."

We all shuffle out of the gym and I see Paloma, Annie, and Sylvie murmuring to each other but I have no idea what they're talking about.

Will's mom picks him up because he has another orthodontist appointment, so I take the late bus home on my own and try not to stress about our assigned groups of three. I feel mostly excited, like three-quarters excited, but then there's one quarter of weird ickiness with Sylvie.

If none of what happened with the sleepover had happened, we would be so happy to be on this committee together, and instead it's like a thick cloud in the air, like when you're driving and see a fire off in the distance and you know something is wrong.

I think about Sylvie and me in the same group. Maybe that would help my mission. I partly pray that we are and then pray that we're not. I can't seem to make up my mind.

I walk into the house and my phone starts vibrating immediately. "Yo," Adelaide says as soon as I answer the FaceTime call. "Happy Friiiiiiday."

She's holding the phone in such a way that I can only see her feet. She's given herself a rainbow pedicure.

"Nice toes." I giggle.

"Thanks! It's all Sharpie. Cool, huh?"

"Um, is that safe? Permanent marker on your skin?" I try not to appear too alarmed.

"It's fine! Len, you're like three hundred and six years old the way you worry about this stuff. Chill, bro."

"Bro?" I laugh again.

She moves the phone super close to her face so all I can see is part of her eyeball. It's a little freaky.

"Soooo," she says. "How's the mission? How was the meeting?"

"I wrote to Charlotte, she wrote me back, and I just wrote her back, and I've been talking to Will more, so that's something." I sigh. "The planning meeting was fine and Sylvie was there and we might get put in a small group together, which kind of terrifies me, but anyway."

"Interesting," she replies. It suddenly gets very loud and I can't hear what Adelaide is saying and she puts the phone down so all I see is ceiling. "I'll text you. They're drilling outside and my head is about to explode."

"K."

Adelaide: Yo

Me: Yo

Adelaide: You never say yo

Me: Hahahah idk

Adelaide: What else happened at the meeting

Me: Not much, was just awk being there with Sylvie and could get more awk idk

Adelaide: Chill, girl

Adelaide: Don't get so bogged down with Sylvie

Adelaide: Almost time for Brenna

Me: Lol you're on top of this

Adelaide: I am and anyway you gotta go big or go home with this mission, girl, just talk to the people and figure this out.

Me: That's hard but ok

Adelaide: I know but I can tell you're super mopey and you need to just take charge with your mission and move forward

Me: How can you tell I'm mopey?

Adelaide: I just can, Len. I know you.

Me: Okay, going to dinner, text later

Adelaide: K. Yum. Bye.

I guess the tiniest silver lining of this whole thing is that Adelaide is kind of moving into the friend-friend category.

Maybe?

THAT NIGHT, MY MOM, DAD, and I go to dinner at Mozzarella Sticks, Longport's best pizzeria, and then we walk over to Longport Cones. I'm so excited about my two scoops of cookies and cream in a pretzel cone, but right when I get inside, I lose my appetite completely.

Sylvie, Zora, Paloma, and Annie are sitting right there, at the booth by the door. Anjali is with them too.

They look up at me and I look back at them and then nothing. Silence.

"Oh, um, hi, Eleni," Paloma says finally, licking the side of her cone and making wide eyes at the others.

"Hi." I freeze and then say, "Oh my God, I forgot something in the car, I gotta go, bye, guys." I run out and forget all about the two scoops of cookies and cream. My parents follow along after me.

They're all together, having fun, and I'm out with my parents on a Friday night? I want to sink into the sidewalk. I'm the biggest loser in the world.

"We need to go home. Now," I tell them.

"Len," my dad says, putting a gentle hand on my shoulder. "I'm sure there's an explanation. Your friends know you always do Shabbat dinner with us."

"Dad." I glare.

"I think what Dad is trying to say is," my mom starts and then hesitates; I see her face getting red, and she starts talking fast. Her fists are clenched. "What he's trying to say is that you always spend Friday nights with us. It's our tradition. They know that."

I ignore that. It's obvious she's saying that more for her than for me even. She wants an excuse. An explanation. She wants something to make it all seem not as bad as it really is. I feel her ramping up, about to lose it. About to get so mad at them for leaving me out that she ends up getting mad at me, too, somehow. I just want to stop her before she gets started. Make it go away. These things always feel like accidentally stepping in wet cement. And then once I'm there, I can't get out. "Come on. We're leaving," I say as quietly as I can.

Under his breath, my dad adds, "I was really looking forward to a mint-toffee cone," but it's in his jokey voice and I don't even respond to it.

On the car ride home, I burst into tears. Nothing is working, nothing feels right, and this whole friendship mission is dumb.

"Leni," my dad says from the front seat, turning his head a bit to look back at me while at a traffic light. "It's gonna be okay. I promise you. Really. It's gonna be okay."

"It's not gonna be okay!" I scream. "I don't have any friends! I didn't have any friends at camp this summer, either! Maddy totally ditched me. I couldn't tell you that because I didn't want you to freak out and call the camp and make everything out of control." I choke back some sobs. "I don't have friends at school. You saw what happened with the sleepover! Even Will barely talks to me! I am alone. Completely and totally alone!"

They're silent then, maybe even speechless, who knows. My mom stares at my dad in this teeth-clenched *what are we going to do with her* way.

"I told you this was an issue, Jake!" my mom says forcefully, lashing out at him. "You don't listen to me. No one listens to me." She pauses for a second. "It's time to consider private school; they offer financial aid. You need to listen to me!" she screams.

I don't understand how she thinks getting agitated when I'm upset and stressed is the answer. There should be a class for moms to take so they can learn what to do when their daughters are upset. It seems like all the other moms figured this out—not mine, though. It's like there's a signal that when Eleni is stressed and struggling, that means my mom needs to struggle and get stressed, too.

No. It should be the opposite.

If I'm going through something, I don't need her emotions on top of it. It's like I'm carrying cinder blocks and then she just adds bricks onto them. All I want to do is put it all down, but somehow I get stuck carrying everything and trying to pretend none of it is heavy at all.

Usually I end up focusing more on her feelings than on mine. Maybe in some way that's a reason I can't keep friendships. I don't know how exactly. I'm not a psychologist. But maybe. The thing is, it always feels like there's no room for my feelings because my mom's take up so much space.

"That's not the answer, Mom," I say finally, softly, not yelling back. I can't rile her up anymore.

Everyone is silent after that, and when we get home, I run up to my room and lie down on my bed in my clothes.

"She's such a good kid, Ruthie. She'll find her way through this," I overhear my dad say. "And the thing is, these struggles are part of growing up."

"You always try to sum things up so neat and tidy, Jake," my mom says. "It's not so simple."

"Ruthie, please, try to listen to me," he says. "I know you're upset, but getting angry won't help."

It gets quiet, but then I do hear another thing—the soft, almost inaudible little sounds of my mom crying. They're more like hiccups or coughs.

Maybe half hiccup, half cough.

Probably the worst sound ever.

FriENDship: Brenna

HEBREW SCHOOL STARTS ON SUNDAY morning.

My dad always drives me because he stays at the temple for the Brotherhood Bagels hangout that takes place during Hebrew school hours. It's sort of the equivalent of my mom's book club, only the men don't read and they basically just sit there drinking coffee and eating bagels and discussing the news or sports or whatever.

I'm out on the deck soaking in a few minutes of early morning sun before it's time to go when my phone starts exploding with texts.

Anjali: I'm really sorry about the Cones thing

Anjali: Sylvie just invited me after art class and I said okay, it wasn't a planned out thing between us.

Anjali: I didn't even know Paloma and Annie and Zora were meeting us there

Anjali: She didn't tell me

Me: Okay.

Anjali: For real don't be mad

Me: I'm fine, it's okay

Me: I gotta get ready for Hebrew

Anjali: Kk talk later

Adelaide: Don't forget to really go there with Brenna today

Me: Kind of impressed you pay that much attention to my schedule

Adelaide: Well, I am your coach

Me: True

Adelaide: Promise you'll just be bold and say what you need to say

Me: Um. I'll try.

I'm medium shocked that Adelaide is so invested in this, but also kind of flattered, too. But of course there's that tiny corner of my brain that says she's forced to do this by her mom. I want to be bold like she says, but at the same time I'm not totally sure I even have it in me to do that. What little bit of confidence I had from the Charlotte letters seems to have evaporated after the Longport Cones debacle.

"Leni!" my dad calls from inside. He doesn't know I'm out here. "Come on, time to go! We're gonna be late."

Me: I gotta go
Adelaide: Kk bye

We get to the temple and my dad parks in his usual spot in the back of the parking lot. We walk in together and he goes to the social hall for bagels and coffee with his pals and I walk through the religious school wing to Classroom Aleph (*Aleph* is the letter A in Hebrew) and take a seat in the back.

I'm the first one here. So much for being late. Not that I was even worried about that. We're never, ever, ever late. For my parents, lateness is the absolute worst quality a person can have.

As I wait for the rest of my class to arrive, I take out my notebook and start to construct the Brenna timeline.

First grade: Brenna Walsin starts Hebrew school at Temple Beth Am and Eleni and Brenna become good friends right away

December of second grade: Brenna and Eleni officially form the union called BrenLen at a Hanukkah party

December—summer before third grade: Friendship is normal and good. We hang out a little outside of Hebrew school but not so much.

Beginning of third grade: Friendship is still fine and good but twins TJ and Bette Isaacson move to Longport and start Hebrew school (was this the beginning of the end? Not sure. TBD)

Hanukkah party in third grade: Brenna declares to Eleni while eating mini latkes that BrenLen is disbanding

Third grade to now: Brenna and Eleni do not speak

I look over the notes for a few more minutes, but when classmates start to come in, I put my journal away so no one sees.

The timeline is okay but I think I need more data, more actual fragments of our friendship to piece together. But then I remember! We did used to text and send each other GIFs from our moms' phones and we thought it was hilarious. We felt so grown up!

My mom saves every single text so I'll need to find a way to get my mom's phone and dig through. Maybe I can sneak onto my mom's email, too, because she was the one who set up playdates with Brenna's mom and made plans for Tot Shabbat gatherings and sukkah hangouts and all the stuff surrounding Jewish holidays.

When Brenna walks in, I start to feel all sneaky, like I'm doing something wrong. But she has no idea she's part of this mission, so yippee—I have nothing to worry about.

She has her hair up in a messy bun and she looks like she woke up three and a half seconds ago. She's still wearing her Ugg slippers and her facial expression sort of screams *Sunday Hebrew is pure torture* like she's not sure she'll survive this day, let alone the whole year.

Brenna doesn't say hi to anyone as she comes in, just plops herself down at the desk a row in front of mine, folds her arms, and rests her head on them.

We spend the first day of Hebrew school doing an all-school program about the IALAC sign. It stands for *I am lovable and capable* but you don't find that out until the end. And it's about all the ways other people can tear pieces off of your IALAC sign.

We talk about how to be kinder and more sensitive to people's needs, and how to look out for others.

At the end of class, we gather our stuff to get ready to go and I hop up from my chair, about to head out. When I pass Brenna's desk, I have to stop and say something. Be bold, or try to, like Adelaide says. "Hey, how was your summer?" My words fall out of my mouth, all choppy-sounding.

She turns to face me. "Uh, hey, Eleni." Her eyes bulge, almost like she's shocked I'm talking to her. "Summer was fine. Went to camp. Our counselor left halfway through though because she was homesick, so that was a little weird." She shrugs.

"Oh, yeah, that is a little weird. Was it her first time away from home?" I ask.

"Ummm, not sure. Eleni, you always ask follow-up questions. Do you know that? Most people would just sort of nod and say yeah."

Suddenly it feels like she walked in on me in a bathroom stall. I don't think she meant the question to be mean, but now I feel like I've been zapped—an unable-to-reply level of embarrassment.

"I guess?" is all I can manage to say.

"No, I mean it's a good thing." She smiles. "Anyway. Hebrew school continues to be THE WORST," she yells as soon as our teacher is out of the room.

We walk out together, not really talking, and I find my dad outside. I don't feel like today was a total failure. Brenna and I started talking. We connected a little. She even gave me a mini compliment.

A teeny tiny step in the right direction.

FriENDship: Brenna continued

IT'S WEDNESDAY AFTER SCHOOL AND I'm on my way to Monterey Springs, where my mom works, because there was a huge plumbing issue at one of Dad's job sites and my mom has a late meeting. I took the bus here because there's a stop pretty close, and also Banana Bread, my favorite bakery in the world, is on the way.

I pick up a chocolate chip muffin for me and a corn muffin for my mom and walk to Monterey Springs. I'll do my homework, try not to stress about this overnight rooming situation, and hopefully dig a little through my mom's phone to move forward with the Brenna part of the mission.

A lot of times when my mom's busy at work she leaves her phone right on her desk while she runs around to deal with various things, so this is kind of perfect. I won't even have to ask her. She won't even know that I'm doing it.

I walk inside and say hello to Manny, the security guy, and then take the elevator up to the third floor to my mom's office.

She's typing and talking on the phone at the same time when I walk in. I open the bag of muffins and break off a piece of mine, passing hers across the desk.

"I understand that. Believe me. The thing is, the waiting list is about three pages long at this point." Pause. "Yes. We are doing everything to get your mother in." Pause. "Yes. Of course. I understand." Pause. "Okay. I will be in touch as soon as possible. Have a good day."

"Hi, Len," she says, distracted and frustrated-sounding. "Things are so crazy, so just do your homework and let me catch up on this pile of work."

I nod.

"I have a meeting in ten minutes. Thank you for this muffin, by the way." She sits back in her chair.

A few minutes and few more calls later, my mom finally opens the bag and breaks off a piece of muffin and pops it into her mouth. "How are things?"

I finish chewing my bite. "Um, fine." I nod to sort of

signal that all is okay and we don't need to keep discussing me or what's going on or anything.

"I'm still furious at Jill," she says, bringing up a topic I obviously don't want to discuss, and just talking about what she wants to talk about.

I stare into my muffin bag and break off another piece. "Yeah. I understand," I say. "But I'm okay."

That's a lie; I'm definitely not okay. And it's so sad I can't tell my mom that or be honest with her. But I can't. I need to just pretend things are fine because it's the only way to make it through. Telling her I'm not okay only makes things harder for me because she gets so upset and always needs a solution to every single thing immediately. She gets so angry when things aren't the way she wants them to be even when it's not her life.

My mom gets another call and then she tells me it's time for her meeting.

Please leave your phone. Please leave your phone. Please leave your phone.

It's sitting right there on her desk, next to the box of tissues, and she's frazzled at the moment, looking for her glasses, so I think there's a good chance she'll totally forget about the phone.

My heart pounds in suspense, like this is the hugest thing that's happened, like I'm literally here waiting to see my fate. She grabs her leave-at-work cardigan and walks out of her office.

Her phone is on the table!

Victory is mine!

I walk around to her side of the desk and grab the phone. It asks me for a password but duh—of course I know what it is. My birthday.

I type it in and the whole phone world opens up. I picture myself strolling through these gigantic golden gates of Phone Land, all the mysteries of the world waiting to be unlocked.

I open up the text messages tab and scroll through all of them. Messages from my dad about grocery shopping, texts with Louisa, of course, because they're pretty much twelve-year-olds who text back and forth a million times a day. Texts with the cleaning lady, and group texts with some of the other moms from the PTA.

I keep scrolling down and finally find a text thread between Melissa Walsin and my mom. Feeling pretty grateful that my mom is adamant about saving all text messages, like she's adamant about saving pretty much everything.

I scroll all the way up to see the beginning of the text chain.

Melissa: Hello! So glad the girls are becoming friendly.

Mom: Me too!

Melissa: Would you like to all come over for Shabbat

dinner Friday?

Mom: Would love to!

Melissa: Great. Bring a side dish and come over around 5

Mom: Perfect

I start to scroll through because so many of these texts are about logistics and making plans and not so much about the friendship itself or anything that took place.

I skip around a little bit and find the back-and-forth between Brenna and me. I don't think I ever added Brenna as a contact to the phone so it's a little hard to find, but I finally do.

Me: Hiiiiii

Brenna: Hiiiiiiiiiiiiiii

Brenna:

Kdlsdkfjsdfjosidfjehsdfsapfsdfjsdlkfjsdjfhsdfh

Me: Skdjfqwnnfnsnsnnqnqnqnqnsspspssjqnqnq

Brenna: Hahahahaha

Me: Hahahahahahahahaahahahahahahahah

Me: Can't wait to come over

Brenna: Do you like slime

Me: I love slime

Brenna: Me too

Brenna: Do you like American girl

Me: Ya

Brenna: Me too

Me: Fun

Brenna: Yaaaaaaaaaaaaaaaaaaa

I slump over the desk a little bit, realizing that none of this is even remotely helpful and I'm literally getting nowhere. I even scroll down to closer to the date when the Hanukkah fiasco took place and there's not much there except a few GIFs of dancing Hanukkah candles and a steaming plate of potato latkes.

This mission is full of exciting brainstorms and then soul-crushing realizations that I'm stopping and starting without any real progress.

I need to call in (I guess text in, in this case) for reinforcement.

Me: Hiiii need your help

Adelaide: I'm doing fine, thanks for asking

Adelaide: Jk

Me: Sorry. How are you?

Adelaide: Fine, fine. What's up?

Adelaide: In the middle of this sci lab & want to cut my toenails off with a steak knife it's that bad

Me: Ewwww

Me: I just keep feeling like I'm not making progress with my mission

Me: And like does Sylvie even miss me?

Adelaide: Maybe u need to just skip the others & talk to her

Me: Idk

Me: Even when I tried to talk to Brenna, I couldn't really figure out what to say

Adelaide: Hmmmm

Adelaide: Did you find any more clues or stuff in your texts with Brenna when u went through your mom's phone

Me: Not really

Adelaide: I AM A GENIUS

Me: ???

Adelaide: !!!

Adelaide: Try searching her name, maybe your mom emailed other people about her

I wonder when Adelaide became such a sleuth or if she was always this way.

Me: Ooh good idea, going to try that

Adelaide: Kk good luck

My heart pounds as I do this; I'm clearly snooping. And what if I find out things I don't want to know, like she's sick or my dad is sick or Pontoon is sick. Anything at all seems to freak me out.

Hi Lou,

Crazy times here, so looking forward to our dinner date next week. This girl Brenna at our temple is making me nuts! Never have I met such a malicious small child. She seems to have it out for Leni and I don't know why. I'm friendly with the mom but not super close. We need to talk; need your advice as usual. Thoughts on New Year's Eve in the Berkshires? Thinking we can stay at that inn again with the girls and sit in the lounge outside our rooms when they go to sleep. Let me know.

xoxo Ruthie

I scroll down to another email, look up for a second, and then I see my mom's head in the doorway.

My heart thumps. I throw the phone down on the desk. "Um, I was checking the time."

She looks at me, confused. "Uh, okay. Len, come with me. Some of the canasta ladies want to see you."

My heart perks up a little. The canasta ladies are my favorite. They've been living here for five years and when they first moved in they started a weekly canasta game. I'd come to work with my mom when she couldn't find babysitting and they'd invite me to sit with them and watch the game. And of course I was into it—mostly for the snacks.

They'd put out a whole spread—grapes and fancy

cheese and all different kinds of crackers, plus fancy pieces of chocolate and sparkling cider.

It was a party every single week.

"Eleni!" Rose squeals when we get downstairs. She's the loudest of the bunch. "You are so tall and gorgeous. Come here. Let me look at you."

My lips curve into the embarrassed kind of smile that only pops up when old ladies comment on your physical appearance.

"What a beautiful young lady," Rita adds. "People pay millions for that shade of brown hair!"

Shirley and Marsha nod in agreement.

"Okay, I'm off to my last meeting of the day," my mom announces. "You'll keep an eye on her, ladies?"

"We sure will!" Marsha sings.

They get started with the game and to be honest, I still don't really understand it even though they've tried to explain it to me so many times.

"So how are you doing, doll?" Shirley asks. "How's school?"

I hesitate a little. "It's a little weird this year, middle school. I'm adjusting, though, I think. Some up-and-down friendships." I'm not even sure why I'm sharing this, but I guess on some level I wonder if they'll have any advice for me.

"We understand up-and-down friendships," Marsha says. "Don't we, ladies?"

"Oh, do we! Remember when Rita ran against me for the school board?" Rose asks the others. "That was a trip!"

"Oh, Rosie, stop already with that." Rita shakes her head. "It's been forty years and you're still going on and on about this. Enough! Dayenu! Enough!"

I giggle at Rita's random use of Hebrew, especially the word *dayenu*, which literally means "enough" and is usually only said at a Passover seder.

They all bicker back and forth about whatever happened with the school board and then Marsha says, "It's not funny to even joke. The worst year of my life when you two weren't speaking. I thought our foursome was done for."

"You did?" Shirley squawks. "I knew these two loons would come around."

"Wait," I jump in. "I think I need to hear more about this."

A firecracker explosion goes off in my brain.

These ladies. My FFFM.

A lifetime of friendship drama right in front of me at this very moment. The canasta ladies can help me figure stuff out! I have Adelaide and she's great, but these ladies can be instrumental in solving the mysteries, too, I think.

Each one of them. All pieces of the puzzle.

"You sure you want to hear about a group of old ladies who had a knock-down, drag-out fight forty years ago?" Rita asks me.

"Kinda, yeah," I say honestly. "Maybe I can learn from you guys?"

All of a sudden, I feel little pinprick tears crawling into the corners of my eyes. I push them back, blinking a few times, forcing them to stay away.

Rose shakes her head and raises a finger in the air. "I'll tell you this. Women's friendships ebb and flow and they are lifelong. Lifelong! Never ending." She looks at her friends. "Should we tell her about Gail and the dining room fiasco?"

"Well, now you have to!" I laugh. "Sounds too intriguing to just toss out there like that."

They all chuckle. "You're funny, Eleni! Do you know that?" Marsha asks me.

"I am?" I giggle in my nervous-embarrassed hard-to-stop way. "Okay. So tell me."

Marsha leans forward onto the table. I guess the card game is on hold for now. "So this woman Gail Farkas just moved in here. She's lovely. Used to live in Hardwick, our kids played soccer together. Anyway. She moves in and she expects to have her first-choice dinner table—with the other ladies from Hardwick who she used to know but has not remained in touch with. But it doesn't work that way. You're placed where you're placed to start and some tables are full. It's just how it is."

"Get to the point, Marsh!" Rose screams and cackle-laughs.

"Anyway, she has a fit. Your mother has to get involved. Her table doesn't change. And she spends every meal complaining to the people how it's injustice and she doesn't want to sit there, and she's not going to stop fighting." Marsha shakes her head. "So, you'll see, even old ladies feel left out."

"Wow." I look at all of them, and it almost feels like a huge boulder sinks from my throat to my toes. I don't want to go through life always worrying about feeling left out. Even when I'm an old lady in a retirement community. At some point this stuff has to get figured out, right? That's what I always thought, what I always expected.

"So what she's saying is," Shirley adds, "it never ends, but it usually gets resolved and ends up torturing you less."

Maybe if everyone embarked on a FFFM, all the friendship drama could get resolved earlier.

"I see." My stomach feels gurgly like when you're swimming in a lake and a gigantic boat passes by and you sort of wobble up and down for a bit. "But what about the school board fight?"

"Oh, here we go," Shirley says.

Rita launches into a whole dissertation. "I said I was running. Then Rose here also decides to run, and there's a whole back-and-forth debate, and people's campaign signs were torn down!" She leans forward. "No one ever found out who did that, by the way. Never. But I have my hunches!"

"They didn't speak for a year," Shirley adds. "Rose won the election. We were all distraught. They mended ways when Rita's son Howie broke his leg and Rose pulled some strings to get the best orthopedist on Long Island to do the surgery."

I sit back in my chair. "This is really some story."

Marsha shakes her head. "It's enough already if you ask me. We're old ladies. We want peace. We don't want to rehash old battles."

"Amen!" Rose raises her hand in the air. "Now, can we please play cards? I have a hair appointment in two hours."

"So you're not coming to lobster night?" Marsha asks.

"I'll be there late! I already told you this, Marsh."

I sit back and observe all of this and their canasta game. I never realized that friendship adjustments and fights and breakups and reunions and all the ups and downs can be lifelong.

I guess the canasta ladies are part of my FFFM now, too.

FriENDship: Sylvie

"ARE YOU LOVING THIS PLANNING committee?" Elizabeth asks me at lunch on Friday. "Or I guess you've only had one meeting, so . . ." She cracks up at herself.

"Yeah, our second meeting is today. We're getting put into small groups. I'm kinda nervous." I take a bite of my turkey wrap and a big gulp of iced tea to swallow it down.

"I heard a lot of people aren't going back for this one," Rumi adds. "The triplets felt like it was gonna be annoying and no one was gonna listen to kids' ideas anyway."

"Oh, really?" I look up at her, my stomach tightening. If a lot of people don't go back, that means Sylvie and I have more of a chance of being in the same group. I can't decide if I want us to be or not. Like if we are, and it feels totally normal and good, maybe we'd take the late bus home together, and really talk, and get somewhere.

But if we are and it's awkward, it might make this whole mission so much harder.

I don't know which way it'll go, and that uncertainty feels me with dread.

"Yeah," Anjali says, and lowers her head to talk to me. "Annie and Paloma aren't going back. Sylvie was crying about it at this special exhibit thing we had to go to with our art class on Wednesday night. She kind of cries a lot."

"She does?" My voice squeaks at the end and I take another sip of iced tea.

"Yeah, her mom is making her go back because she thinks she made a commitment to it or something, and the teachers will think less of her if she quits, even though it's not really like that." Anjali shrugs. "Anyway, so much drama over nothing, right?"

I nod. "Yeah, seems that way." I finish the last bite of my wrap. "Sure none of you want to come with me today?" I wide-smile with my teeth clenched, a facial expression that pretty much says I'm begging.

"So sorry, Len," Elizabeth replies. "I really can't. My parents refuse to let me miss a single tennis lesson because the makeup policy is so bad."

"Same with Indian dance," Anjali adds, frowning.

"Yeah, and honestly I'm just not a committee kind of gal." Rumi smooshes up her face. "No offense, though,

Len. It's not that I don't want to be with you."

I nod and half smile. "Okay, at least there's that."

I shuffle back and forth between feeling relieved Paloma and Annie aren't going back to feeling scared that I'll be alone with Sylvie. The rest of the day goes in slow motion and I just want it to be the meeting time already, so I can get it over with.

Finally, the day ends and I head over to the gym. People are already there, sitting at the table, chatting and doodling. I take a seat on the opposite side from Sylvie and I try to really observe her while not making it obvious that I'm observing her.

She doesn't make eye contact with me at all, like she really has no idea I'm here. For some reason, she came looking super official today, with a clipboard, like she's in charge or something. She has these tortoiseshell glasses now and they make her look super old and mature. It kind of freaks me out.

I keep glancing toward the door to see if Annie and Paloma are going to come running in. Maybe they're late; maybe there's a chance they're still coming and Anjali got it wrong.

"So all the plans your teachers are making for the overnight are truly excellent." Ms. Baldour looks down at her notes. "I know there have been some rumors circulating about the rooming situation and we're still sorting that out. What I really want to nail down today is for each group to come up with three things they'd like to see happen while we're at the retreat center."

I look around the table and people start raising their hands, reaching out, like they really need to be called on.

"Yes?" She looks over at Juliette.

"Hi, um, I just want to say that since we're on this committee, we should have input on the rooming, and I'm really uncomfortable rooming with someone I don't know." She pauses. "Um, yeah."

"Thanks for the input, Juliette." Ms. Baldour smiles. "But we need to move forward with the ideas from this—"

"Ms. Baldour," Fara Shae calls out, interrupting her. "I'm really sorry to interrupt, but honestly I think people should get to pick one person to room with and then if we're not with them, we should at least be near them, like on the same hall. . . . I mean, it's just a really emotional time, and I think our feelings should be taken into consideration. And, um—"

"Thank you, Fara." Ms. Baldour clears her throat. "Again, we're going to move on from this."

"Please, please, please let us room with friends," Ashley Philbrick pleads.

"Ashley. Enough." Ms. Baldour gives Ashley a look that says *you must stop talking immediately.*

There's a little grumbling after that and a few people shaking their heads, but Ms. Baldour ignores it. She looks out at all of us. "When I say ideas, I mean things like writing get-well cards for children in the hospital, some getting-to-know-you games; we can come up with a school-wide community service project to do when we're back, pretty much the sky's the limit. I was going to discuss this as a big group, but there's been too much calling out and interrupting. Each small group should write down three things and then submit them to me, and the faculty and I will discuss."

She looks down at her notes again and starts to read out the groups. "Josh Fanzin, Lily McKnight, Will Spinick, you can go over there to the left-hand corner of the gym. Melissa Samuelson, Evie Conklin, Juliette Belsoni, head on over the right corner. "Eleni Klarstein." My heart is the loudest drum in the world right now. I'm shocked the whole table isn't turning to look at me because they can hear it. "Abe Melman." Gulp. "Sylvie Bank."

My stomach drops like I'm on a Guinness World Records roller coaster. After that, I stop listening to the other groups. I don't even know where I'm supposed to go. I just get up when it's time and follow Abe.

"Hey, Eleni." Abe turns around. "Do you still want to open a stationery store?"

My eyes bulge. "You remember that? We haven't been in the same class since fourth grade."

"I'd never forget it." He nods. "Remember I told you that you should also have a cooler because people are always thirsty at stores and want drinks?"

I laugh for a second. "Yeah, I do remember that."

Abe is a goofy kid who's always talking about food and brings half-sour pickles as his lunch snack. He has shaggy black hair and giant brown eyes and he kind of looks like a human teddy bear.

If there was one person who could ease any tension with Sylvie and me, it would definitely be Abe.

We get to our corner of the gym and Sylvie doesn't even glance at me. She plops herself down, sitting on her backpack, texting (even though we're not supposed to have phones out at school) and looking annoyed.

"So, lovely group," Abe starts, clearing his throat, like ahem, Sylvie, put your phone away. "What are our ideas? We gotta make this fast. My uncle is in town and we're going out for deli."

"Abe, it's only three thirty p.m.," I remind him.

"Yeah, my great-uncle. He needs to eat dinner by four thirty or who knows what'll happen."

I smile. "Got it."

I look over at Sylvie while she's still angry-texting and I don't expect her to meet my gaze, but then she glances up and we make eye contact and then I quickly look away. Of course we have a million ideas; we've only been talking about this for three years now.

"I definitely think we should do that thing where one person starts a story and the rest of the group has to go around, finishing it, person by person," I say. Sylvie doesn't look up this time, even though we used to do that every day at Longport Day Camp. It was our favorite.

"And I think we need to have a how-big-can-you-make-a-sandwich contest," Abe adds. "Like how many things can we put on it. Lettuce, tomato, tuna, turkey, cheese, pickles, olives, all the condiments . . . I could go on."

I slow-nod. "Interesting. We may be at the mercy of the chef for that one. . . ."

"Sylvie?" Abe says, looking at her. I wonder where her clipboard went.

"Let's do that thing where you have to dress your teacher up like a mummy," she says finally, smiling. "Remember when we had that idea, Leni? We saw it on some show."

My heart bubbles up. "Yes, it looked awesome."

"Oh, wait," I add. "What about that game Ruby told us about *How well do you know your teacher?*"

"OMG, yes!" Sylvie laughs. "I forgot about that but now I remember!"

My heart expands like someone blowing up a giant pool float.

"Oh, Leni, remember how we wanted do a cookie-cake-eating contest at my party in fourth grade but my mom said no?"

I nod all fast. "Yes! That would be SO fun as a grade."

"Love that one!" Abe sings. "Okay, writing all of these down. We are on fire!" Abe sings again. "Anything else?"

"No. Honestly, I think I need to leave," Sylvie says, her mood changing abruptly. "I don't really want to be on this committee anymore, who even knows if they're going to pick these ideas."

I'm so surprised I don't even know what to say. Nothing happened at all.

"I think they will," Abe answers. "I'm also going to add that we should all paint self-portraits, too."

"Sounds good," I answer, deflated from Sylvie's mood shift.

At this point, Sylvie stops paying attention. She texts the rest of the meeting until Ms. Baldour says it's time to pack up and head to the late bus or out to the pickup line for whoever is picking us up.

She grabs her backpack and slings it over her shoulder and doesn't say goodbye to Abe or me. She's the first one to leave the gym.

"I thought you and Sylvie were best friends?" Abe asks me, bending down to tie his shoelace.

I shrug. "It's complicated." I honestly don't understand what just happened. For a moment, it almost seemed like old times between us, and then zap—she was angry and distant and mean again.

"A can't-live-with-her, can't-live-without-her kind of thing?" Abe asks as we leave the gym.

"I guess you could say that."

20

IT'S BEEN A FEW DAYS since the planning meeting and Sylvie and I are back to not making eye contact again. We had that brief moment of connection with all of our old ideas and then she just left. It made no sense.

We're about to be off from school for Rosh Hashanah so they make us do a locker cleanout last period, to make sure that half-eaten lunches don't get abandoned in the lockers during our time away, making everything stinky and disgusting when we get back. This may be primarily for Abe Melman because of his half-sour pickle obsession.

My locker is still neat, though, which makes the whole thing even worse. It's just more time for me to stand around and feel awkward near Sylvie and the rest of them.

I sit here on the floor with my back to the locker and pretend to be really engrossed in *Number the Stars*. Usually I am, it's an amazing book, but right now I've had to read the same page four times because my eyes are scanning the words but I'm not taking in anything I'm reading.

I pretend to ignore Sylvie, Annie, and Paloma, who are doing some kind of Rockettes-style kickline in the middle of the hallway, not cleaning their lockers at all. I'm really good at pretending; I don't even look up from my book. I only see them out of the sides of my eyes.

"Oh! I have to tell you something," Sylvie yelps when they stop dancing. She taps Paloma on the shoulder and whispers something in her ear.

"Oh, okay, yeah," Paloma replies. "Totally."

I still pretend I don't see it or hear it or even know they're here. But there are three hundred razor blades in my throat; it takes all of my energy to make sure I don't burst into tears right here, right now.

"Eleni!" I hear someone call from down the hall.

"We came to visit you at your locker," Elizabeth says when they all get to me.

"Yay! Hi!" Their locker section is in the wing behind mine, but I guess their lockers are clean, too. "I can't believe you all have a day off from school, like a vacation, and I have to sit in temple."

"Sorry, Eleni." Rumi shrugs. "It's your new year but it's

not like a party, right?"

"Right," I answer. "It's confusing. I don't hate it, I like it, but it is a day of being quiet and paying attention to stuff in clothes that aren't the most comfortable."

"The Korean New Year is a little confusing, too, because it's three days long and that's when we celebrate getting a year older even though it's not really our birthday," she muses.

I nod. "That's interesting."

"I want to celebrate every person's new year," Elizabeth adds. "They're all cool! I just get regular New Year's Eve."

"Our new year is pretty much just a celebration of light," Anjali adds.

"Ooh, like Hanukkah is for us," I say.

I love to hear about other people's traditions and I'm super into this chat, but truthfully I'm also just so grateful that they're here with me, and I have people to talk to, and I'm not sitting here alone while Annie, Paloma, and Sylvie dance around me.

Finally, the bell rings and I grab my backpack and I say goodbye to Elizabeth, Rumi, and Anjali and head to the bus.

That night, we have chicken cutlets and roasted potatoes and green beans for dinner. Of course apples and honey, too, the tradition for a sweet new year. And then we get dressed up for Rosh Hashanah evening services. I wear my favorite black-and-white houndstooth dress and my black patent-leather ballet flats.

On our way into temple, I scan the crowd for Brenna, with an embarrassed feeling floating above my head. I shouldn't feel embarrassed, though, since from her perspective, nothing is going on and nothing has changed. All that happened is that we talked once for a few minutes after we hadn't talked in a really long time.

The greeters hand us the sturdy blue prayer books and little pamphlets with announcements and blurbs about upcoming events, and the ushers guide us to our seats. Little huddles of teenagers from the youth group hang out outside the sanctuary, laughing and looking over their shoulders for other friends to join them. They seem so grown up and settled. It feels like that's a million years away for me.

My parents and I sit on the left-hand side in the middle of the sanctuary and at first everyone is stirring, talking to each other, but then the rabbis and the cantor come onto the bimah, the stage at the front of the sanctuary, and the organ music starts and everyone quiets down.

Even though this is technically the Jewish New Year, it's a somber day. It's one of those things about Judaism that really doesn't make much sense. I guess even in our celebrations, we always take some time to think and reflect on how to be better people.

Ten minutes into the service, Brenna, TJ, and Bette traipse in, and for some reason the ushers seat them in the row right in front of us. Brenna nods in my direction when she sees me; she half smiles and half waves and then sits down.

I guess that's something; she acknowledged me at least.

"They shouldn't be sitting on their own, without parents," my mom says to me in a loud whisper, loud enough that people down our row turn their heads.

"Shh," I say back. "Stop."

"Don't tell me what to do, Eleni!" she hisses.

I don't respond. My whole body tightens up like I'm suddenly a stone statue. I force myself to focus on the service, and the prayers and the singing.

I tune out the all-over stinging feeling I get when my mom says stuff like that. I ignore Brenna and TJ and Bette laughing together, heads close, their feet up on the pews.

"I can't stand how they're behaving," my mom loud-whispers again, first to my dad and then to me. I ignore it.

Then the rabbi comes to the podium to start her sermon and the three of them hustle out of the row and leave the sanctuary, quiet, heads close, laughing together.

My mom shakes her head. "Terrible."

I agree with her but I'd never admit that. I also would never admit that even though she's right, that their behavior is terrible, I still want to be a part of that—the heads-close laughing, the feeling of being with friends, away from parents. The feeling of being part of something.

It keeps coming back to me again and again; I can't escape it. I want to be part of something, part of a group that actually makes sense. I know I have Anjali, Rumi, and Elizabeth kind of, but it feels forced, not completely right.

I want to feel like I belong somewhere. Now I'm just a lonely kayaker in a lake of full canoes.

"Shanah tovah, everyone," Rabbi Fink starts. "It's wonderful, as always, to see you all here. I'm going to get right to it." She pauses. "I was worried for a while there that you were all forgetting the thing you learned over and over again—at summer camp, religious school, from your parents and grandparents." She pauses again. "You're not required to complete the work to make the world a better place. But you are not free to abandon it altogether. Loose translation from the Hebrew. I was worried that you were all going to abandon the task of making the world a better place when things got hard. And we all know they've been hard." She looks out at the congregation. "When things are hard, we shouldn't turn inward. No, the opposite. We should turn outward. Look to our communities, help when we can, open ourselves up, not close ourselves off."

She goes on and on and I listen to her words. I think about what she's saying in terms of empathy and generosity and kindness.

And then I think about myself, too. And what all that means for me.

"We need to show up," Rabbi Fink continues. "I think if you go through life with that simple phrase in the back of your mind, it can take you far, almost as far as you need to go. Show up for your places, for your community, for your people. Show up the way all of them have shown up for you. Think about what showing up means for you. Does it mean to help, volunteer, listen to the needs of others? All of the above."

Show up. I keep hearing that phrase echo in my head for the whole rest of the service and I keep trying to sum up how that applies to me and my FFFM.

I know it applies. I just don't know how yet.

FriENDship: Charlotte, continued

A FEW DAYS LATER, I get home from school and there's another letter in our mailbox from Charlotte. My heart jumps a little when I see it. She writes back so fast!

Dear Eleni,

So sorry about the thing with Sylvie! That sounds really terrible. I had a similar thing happen last year. This girl Ainsley who always sat in front of me was kind of like my best friend in school even though we didn't hang a ton outside of school and then one day she just became best friends with this other girl Kyla because they were both obsessed with Dance Moms. It was really weird and I'm still kind of confused about it.

Is it so funny we're still writing letters when we could be texting or even calling or FaceTiming? Hee hee. But I love seeing all of your amazing stationery. I am so excited for Halloween. My neighbor who's like sixty but doesn't have kids is making a haunted house for all the kids in the neighborhood. She's so cool and doesn't seem old. I'll try to send you pictures. That overnight sounds really fun and I'm sure you'll have an amazing time but I get that it's hard to imagine without your BFF. Of course it is!

Thanks for being so speedy with replying to my letters!

XOXOXOXO Charlotte

I put her letter in my top desk drawer and promise myself that I'll write back to her later today.

I go downstairs, grab an apple from the fridge, scoop Pontoon up and head out to the porch.

I need to call Adelaide so I can tell her how fired up I'm feeling. The Charlotte letters, the rabbi's sermon, getting ready to talk to Brenna again, even speaking up at the committee meeting with Sylvie—I feel more secure with this mission now. I'm making progress, and I want to tell her face-to-face, even if it is through a screen.

"Hey!" I say, sounding cheerier than I've felt in a while.

"Hey," she grumbles; all I can see is her chin.

"What's wrong?" I ask.

"Pearl Mosley accused me of cheating off her for the math test, which is literally the dumbest since she's not smart at all and I would def never cheat off her, but whatever. My parents had to come in for a meeting and now I'm in trouble. AGAIN."

"But you didn't do anything," I remind her, as if I know the whole story, which I clearly don't. There's music playing in the background and it's a little hard to hear her.

"Yeah, but it doesn't matter. I've been caught cheating before, so I guess once a cheater, always a cheater, who even knows." She pauses and rubs her eye and if I didn't know Adelaide better I would think she's crying, but she's definitely not a crier.

"I'm sorry, Adelaide. Is there any way to prove it?" I deflate a little, wondering if I should hold off on talking about the mission right now.

"I don't know. Maybe. They're going over the tests side by side, so hopefully they see that I DID NOT HAVE ONE SINGLE ANSWER OF HERS BECAUSE SHE IS SO DUMB AND I WOULD NEVER CHEAT OFF HER." She screams the last part so loud it echoes in my eardrums.

"I feel hopeful about that, then," I say. "They'll realize they made a mistake. For sure."

"Maybe. Whatever. Everyone at my stupid school is so stressed all the time, and they're all always looking for someone to blame and I hate it." She puts the phone down and all I see is black. I hear sniffles in the background but I pretend I don't. Now I'm pretty convinced that she really is crying.

"Anyway, enough about stupid me and stupid Pearl and my stupid school." She clears her throat. "What's new with you?"

I finish chewing my bite of apple. "Well, actually I'm feeling sort of good about the FFFM. I got another letter back from Charlotte! I feel like she really gets me."

"Cool." She rolls her eyes. "Sorry I can't be more excited. Literally impossible for me right now."

She turns down the music a moment later and we sit there silently on the FaceTime call and then she tells me she has to go.

"It's okay." I pause. "So. Um, okay, good luck with the whole school thing."

"Yeah. Whatever. Bye."

I sit there for a few seconds after that, feeling kinda blindsided by the conversation and a little worried about Adelaide. I wonder if I should have done more to help her.

Our "friendship" or whatever it is feels a little one-sided, which kind of makes sense given the fact that she was basically forced to be my friend. But even still, maybe I can do more.

Before bed that night, I take out a piece of my tie-dye stationery, one of my favorites, and write back to Charlotte.

Dear Charlotte,

How are you?

I was thinking how cool it would be if we could arrange a reunion one day. I know it would involve flights and stuff but how fun!!!

Do you remember that time we went on the field trip to the bike store in preschool? And then we made that class art project with old bicycle parts? I think that kid Dylann's parents (remember he had 2 n's in his name and we thought that was extra special) ended up winning it at the auction.

Sometimes I think I am sooo weird that I remember all this stuff but it seems like you do too, so that's awesome.

Write back soon!

XOXOXO Eleni

I put on a LOVE stamp and lick and address the envelope, and then I realize something.

I've completed step one!

Charlotte and I are real-life friends again; we only grew apart because we were five years old when she moved.

And then I realize something else too. Something I'm going to do for the rest of this mission.

Every time I finish a FriENDship, I'm going to write the person a letter in my journal. It'll be like a check mark for me, proof that I've finished one step and I'm moving on to the next one.

They're not letters for mailing; they're for saving, for myself, so I can see how far I've come.

I think a big part of life is realizing the process of stuff and your journey, and little signs of success along the way.

Cheering yourself up and giving yourself pats on the back is a big part of it, too.

FriENDship: Brenna, continued

WE MISS A WEEK OF Hebrew school because of where Yom Kippur falls, but now we're back and of course I'm the first one in class like always.

I'm sitting at my desk in the classroom doodling in my journal and brainstorming names for my stationery store. There's also a rapid-fire group text going on between Elizabeth, Rumi, Anjali, and me. We still don't have an official name for our group but the group text name is AnRuEleEli. It's actually kind of catchy.

We're not supposed to have phones out during Hebrew but since no one else is here yet, it feels okay.

Elizabeth: GUYS MY GRANDMA IS COMING TO

STAY WITH US FOR A WHOLE MONTH AFTER HER
SHOULDER SURGERY

Rumi: OMG

Elizabeth: I HAVE TO MOVE OUT OF MY ROOM
AND SLEEP IN THE BASEMENT

Anjali: 😟

Elizabeth: WHAT AM I GOING TO DO?

Rumi: First stop typing in all caps

Rumi: Number one rule of texting

Elizabeth: Blargh

Anjali: Blaaaaaaaargh

Rumi: Bllllaaaaaaarrrrgggggghhhh

I'm typing out a reply when I hear someone coming in; I rush to put my phone in my backpack so I don't get in trouble.

It's Brenna.

My heart pounds. This is a sign. Every other week Brenna is the absolute last person to arrive, but today she's early like me.

"Hey," I stammer as Brenna walks into the classroom.

"Hey," she grumbles back, and takes a seat in the row next to me. "Not in the mood for this. I'm never in the mood for this."

She folds her arms on the desk and lays her head down.

We sit there silently for a few minutes and all I hear

is the loudest ticking clock in the history of clocks. It's hanging above the door. Tick. Tick. Tick. I can't take it anymore. I have to say something.

"Brenna, I have been meaning to tell you," I start, and she picks her head up a little bit, but not completely. "I was bored the other day and I started reading the texts we used to send each other back and forth on our moms' phones."

"We were such lovable little dorks," she says. It feels like a teeny tiny plant has sprouted in my soul that she thinks of both of us as lovable little dorks and that she remembers our friendship, how we used to be.

Not that she deserves it after the third-grade Hanukkah Party fiasco. She doesn't, but it was also almost three years ago. She could have changed by now. That's part of the mission, too, I think. Realizing that people change over time, and friendships change, too, I guess. Obviously my friendship with Charlotte now is way different than it was in preschool.

"I hate this class," Brenna grumbles.

"Yeah," I say, and then regret it because I don't hate the class. I actually don't mind it at all. I love hearing Jewish stories and learning the prayers and how to read and write Hebrew. I'm starting to realize how many times I just agree with people to keep the conversation flowing or tell little white lies to smooth things over. "It's so early in the morning."

"And so boring," Brenna mumbles, and puts her head back down.

I silently pray that her friends are late today and that maybe we'll keep going with this barely-there connection. Maybe I can build on it each week.

"Also TJ and Bette got moved to the other section because of the whole thing that happened in the bathroom at the break-fast after Yom Kippur." Brenna keeps talking like I know the story when I have absolutely no idea what she's referring to. But my teeny tiny plant sprouts even further! She's separated from her friends.

The Meanie Trio (my name for them) is no longer a trio! At least not during Hebrew school, but that's enough for me!

"It's so dumb because Robert Shepsman dared us to do it and I didn't really want to and then Bette was like it's fine and then we all got in trouble." She shakes her head. "Anyway, now I can't hang out with my friends for like a month and I hate Robert Shepsman and he barely got in trouble."

"That sounds really terrible, Bren," I say. "Brenna, I mean."

"So bad." She shakes her head. "I hate everything."

"Sorry to say, but I don't totally know what happened. You may not want to rehash it but, anyway, figured I'd let you know that I don't know." I turn away from her a little bit, wishing I didn't sound so silly.

She sits up with force and turns to face me. My heart pounds, scared she's going to say something mean. "Robert Shepsman saw Bette putting on this lip crayon thing she was obsessed with, like she put it on all day long during the service and then even during break-fast, like every time it rubbed off on her napkin she put on more."

"Okay . . ." I nod, getting her to continue with the story.

"Anyway, he dared Bette, TJ, and me to draw hearts all over the boys' bathroom with the stupid lip crayon when everyone was still in the social hall stuffing their faces after fasting all day." She shakes her head. "I thought it was such a dumb idea because obviously we'd get caught and hello, we had just spent all day atoning for our sins! So I said I wouldn't do it but then they made me stand guard and so I was *complicit* or whatever and so I'm in trouble, too." She puts her head down on the desk again. "And I had to come to the temple an hour early to help staple papers and stuff envelopes. Part of my punishment. And I'm so tired. And I hate everyone." She turns her head the other way. "I feel like I've lost all my friends because of this stupid dare and this stupid lip crayon. Even the words lip crayon make me want to gag."

"That's really frustrating," I reply.

We sit there in silence, listening to the clock again.

"Brenna, I need to say something, so just hear me out, K?"

She eye-bulges, sort of looking scared. "Wait. Please don't tell me you were the one who ratted us out."

I hesitate a second, medium offended she'd think that of me, and also I clearly just told her I had no idea what happened. But I press forward.

"No. I had no idea about any of that." I sit back in my chair. "I just feel like we're older now and it's been a while since we talked, and, like." I hesitate, wanting to stop, but I force myself to continue. "Did I do something that really annoyed you in third grade? I mean, um, why did you just stop wanting to be friends with me?"

She looks at me like my whole face has turned into one giant eyebrow.

"Ummmmmm. Wow. Not what I was expecting and wow, so, ummm. Yeah." She pauses. "I guess? Well, um."

We're silent then and my brain is blank. I can think of zero things to say.

Finally, she starts talking again. "I know I was a mean girl back in the day. My sister literally calls me *little miss mean girl.*"

"She does?" I ask.

"Yeah, she's rude and thinks she's soooo cool, but anyway." She cranes her neck toward the door, I guess to see if anyone is coming. "I'm sorry I was mean to you. I know when Bette and TJ moved here it felt like a big deal for some reason, and I guess I got caught up in that, since, like, you and I have known each other since the Orange

Room, so I sort of wanted to have new friends by third grade. But yeah, it wasn't great of me." She pauses again. "I'm sorry."

I sit back in my chair, a little frozen, like, okay, I dipped a toe, or I guess a leg or probably half my body in the pool, but now I don't know where to go from here or what to say.

"So it wasn't anything I did?" I ask, hesitant.

"Oh my goodness, Eleni!" She bursts out laughing. "This was third grade! I have no idea. I can barely remember last week. Also, like, eight-year-olds aren't really thinking about this kind of stuff. What are you talking about right now?"

I laugh a little, embarrassed but calm. I can't exactly tell her about the mission, even though I kinda want to. Maybe one day.

"Just kinda thinking about some old friendships. Wondering what happened and stuff." I leave it at that.

"Well, we're cool. I mean, I'm in major trouble, but you and me—we're cool. You're like toast, it's impossible not to like you."

I'm not sure if that's really a compliment, but in a way, I think it is. I decide I can check Brenna off the list when I get home. I'll write her a letter and tuck it away.

Step three: complete!

Soon, the rest of the class comes in and I feel kinda

guilty for thinking this, but maybe it's a good thing that the whole lip crayon bathroom incident happened because I actually got to talk to Brenna, and Bette and TJ aren't in our class anymore, so maybe Brenna and I can actually become real friends again.

After Hebrew, I run up to my room to call Adelaide and tell her how I really opened up and talked to Brenna.

I try three times. No answer.

So then I text.

Me: Hey where are you? Call meeeeeee

Still no answer.

I wait a few seconds and then I write the list on a fresh new page of my journal and then my Brenna FriENDship complete letter.

FFFM list

- Charlotte from preschool—writing letters—PEN PALS! COMPLETE!
- Brenna from Hebrew school—TALKED! COMPLETE!
- Will from across the street—working on this
- Maddy from camp—TBD
- Sylvie. Duh. TBD

Dear Brenna,

So I guess what I'm realizing is that the people we were in third grade aren't the people we are today. And also that little kids can be mean without really knowing why. And also that it's good to just talk to people and ask questions and smooth things out sometimes. I'm proud of myself for bringing it up. That was hard for me but I did it. And now we can sort of have a new and improved version of our friendship. Kind of like when they do a reboot of an old TV show. That's what it reminds me of.

Love, Eleni

FriENDship: Maddy

"ADELAIDE'S PHONE'S BEEN TAKEN AWAY," my mom says, like a declaration, on the way home from Monterey Springs a few days later.

"Huh? Why?" She pulls me out of my deep-in-thought moment.

"Her punishment for the cheating incident," she explains.

"But she didn't cheat. That whole thing was made up," I tell her.

"Eleni. I don't know. I have enough of my own stress. I was just telling you in case you were trying to reach her." She grips the steering wheel. I roll my eyes, thankful she can't see me with her focus on the road ahead.

I want to defend Adelaide and say how this whole thing is a mistake, but there's no use. My mom won't listen anyway. I always daydream about what it would be like to have a different mom. Someone who listens, someone who's calm, someone who's able to separate her own stress from the rest of life. Someone who can focus on her daughter and really care in a relaxed, supportive kind of way. Someone who makes things easier for her daughter, not harder.

I wish I had a mom who never spread any of her own drama onto her kid. Like, yeah, she struggles, and everyone goes through stress, but I wouldn't know anything about it at all.

In my dream-world mom, all of her attention would be on me and what I'm going through.

I think I'd be a completely different person if I had a mom like that. I could probably climb Mount Everest on the first try, make it to the Olympics, run for president one day! It's almost too overwhelming to imagine.

My mom and I are quiet for the rest of the ride, and I spend some time thinking about the mission. I'm determined to really focus on Maddy now. She's next on the list, and I'm ready. This FriENDship feels emotional and recent and hard, but I'm ready to tackle it.

I get home and run upstairs and I start to pore through this notebook full of the letters that Maddy and I wrote and mailed to each other.

I wonder if Maddy has the letters I wrote to her over the years, and if she ever looks at them. I wonder if she looked at them before this summer and felt little pangs of weirdness. Maybe she planned to ditch me this summer. Or maybe it just happened.

I guess that's a major thing to figure out.

Maddy & Eleni's NOTEBOOK of BEST BEST BEST CAMP FRIENDSHIP

Summers at Lake Buel Camp aka the BEST BEST BEST camp in the whole entire world.

Now and Forever Until Eternity

I laugh at the fact that we were so sure about eternity when we started this—the summer before fourth grade—and our friendship didn't even last three summers. Maybe we jinxed it with our confidence. The thing is, I was confident it would last forever. I still sort of am, in a way.

Of all the friendships, Maddy is the one that can really be revitalized, I think because we actually chose each other—all on our own at camp. Our moms weren't friends before we were born; we weren't forced together by Hebrew school or by house location.

And, yeah, okay, Brenna and I are on our way to being

friends again. But she's only a Hebrew school friend, not regular school. I don't see her every day or spend whole summers with her.

It's unlikely we'll ever really be first-choice friends, real, true undeniable BFFs. And I'm okay with that.

Part of the FFFM is realizing the role certain friends have in your life—they're not all the same.

I start at the beginning of the letters.

> Dear Eleni,
>
> I am soooo glad we met this summer. You are the funniest person. You are also so wacky. I can't believe you put the spaghetti on your head.
>
> Love, Maddy

I only vaguely remember this, and to be fair it was plain spaghetti, not with sauce, so it was pretty easy to get out of my hair. But even still. Kind of a weird move.

The first batch of letters are all really short, with all kinds of misspellings.

> Dear Eleni,
>
> Your a great freind. Hope we can share a bunk bed next sumer.
>
> Miss you. Love, Maddy

I speed-read them all but then skip ahead to get to the more recent letters. We didn't do as much letter writing before this past summer because we FaceTimed and texted and stuff. But we did have a pact to write to each other at least once a month.

Dear Eleni,

How are you? I have exciting news! I made the travel soccer team. I am obsessed. We play different teams all over the East Coast. It's super cool. We're going to Maine this weekend. Some of the kids say I shouldn't go back to camp and I should go to soccer camp with them but I don't think I'm gonna do that. I'm definitely going to sign up for intercamp soccer though. Would you want to try it with me?

Miss ya! Love, Maddy

Dear Eleni,

Hiiiii! I know what you mean. Not everyone likes soccer. I didn't even know I liked it until recently but now I am obsessed. How are things for you? What's new? Have you been at the beach a lot? I know you and your family like winter beach walks with Pontoon.

Any new names for the stationery store? ☺ Hee hee.

I still like **Does anyone have a pen I could borrow?**
I know it's long though. But does that happen in your
school? Seems like no one ever has a pen or pencil. Do
they vanish into the universe? I don't know.
Bye!

Love, Maddy

Dear Eleni,

One-month countdown to camp! Have you started
packing? I haven't. But my mom ordered me a new
shower caddy and some new sweatpants. I want to get
one of those clip-on lights that change colors.
I haven't gotten a letter from you for last month but
I didn't want to break the pact so I am writing again.
Don't forget to write me! I'll remind you on text.

Love, Maddy

That was the last letter I got before camp this summer, and it makes my heart sink like a gigantic rock at
the bottom of a lake. I don't think I ever sent my last two
monthly letters.

At that time, I was really focused on the fifth-grade
end-of-year stuff and our first dance and the graduation party Sylvie and I were begging our moms to plan
for us.

All these memories come rushing back to me. Maybe Maddy felt like I didn't care. She did ask me to try soccer, and I said no.

Maybe she thought *I* didn't want to be friends with *her*?

FriENDship: Will. Again. ☺

A FEW DAYS LATER, I'M at lunch and I realize that I'm experiencing a strange sort of feeling. The lunch-pit-in-my-stomach that I usually feel isn't there today. I still wish I was over there with Sylvie, Paloma, Zora, and Annie. I still want to get Sylvie back, of course. I still feel completely and totally freaked out about this overnight.

But this minute, I feel kind of fine with Anjali, Rumi, and Elizabeth. Not dancing on the table, cheering, happy beyond belief. But fine. Not like these are my friends for life fine. But fine. Fine for now fine.

Sometimes being fine for now, even if it's not forever, is all that really matters. It's enough to take you through.

I don't know if it's because I've gotten used to things

here or because I'm starting to feel closer to them. I want to talk to Adelaide about all this but she still doesn't have her phone.

Like just now Rumi opened up about her grandma in Korea, who is very sick, and they're trying to get her to move here. And I listened and responded and said maybe my mom could help since she has so much experience with old people.

And then Rumi said, "Oh wow, that's such a good idea. Thank you, Leni."

Right then, it sort of felt like my heart turned a different color, lit up in a bright neon pink.

I leave the cafeteria and I'm walking down the hall to get to science when I see Shai sitting on the bench outside the sixth-grade teachers' office, still eating his lunch.

"Hey, Shai," I say, a burst of confidence popping up out of nowhere. "What are you doing here?"

He looks up from his wrap. Tuna salad, I think. Sort of an odd choice for the middle of the hallway, but I eat cold eggplant pizza some days, so who am I to judge?

"I have math extra help with Mr. Karinsky," he says. "Waiting for him to get off a call."

"Ah. Okay."

"What are you doing?" he asks me after a bite of tuna. I back up, a few steps away from him. I have a dreaded fear of tuna salad from Shai's mouth landing on me.

"Just walking to science." I shrug.

He looks up at me like he just remembered something and wants to finish chewing really fast so he can get the words out. "I was at Will's the other day and his mom is obsessed with those Apple TV slideshows. Know what I mean?"

"Yeah. I love those." I smile.

"All these pics came on of you and Will! I had no idea you were friends since you were babies."

"Um, yeah, well, he's lived across the street from me for, um, forever basically." I pull my hair back into a ponytail, suddenly feeling hot and uncomfortable. "Do you think we can be close like that again?" I ask him, and then instantly regret it. I have no idea why I just asked him that. I mean, I know why—for the mission—but it really seems very odd. I see that now.

"Um." His face turns bright red. "I have no clue. I guess so? Yeah. I mean. Why not?"

I fold my arms across my chest and then put my hands on my hips and then wish I could chop them off because it seems I can't find a comfortable place to put them right now!

A minute later, Shai's called in for math extra help and I keep walking to class. I hadn't realized how hard it is to talk to people. It's like the simplest thing—moving your mouth and having words come out. But it isn't as easy as it sounds. Not for me, anyway.

I get home from school later that day and see that I have three missed FaceTime calls from Adelaide.

"Hey! You have your phone back!" I say as soon as she answers. "Hallelujah," I start singing, and then she cuts me off.

"Yeah. Finally." She rolls her eyes. "Nice that you tried so hard to reach me!"

"What do you mean?" I gasp. "I texted and FaceTimed a zillion times."

"Eleni." She brings the phone close to her face so all I see is eyeball. "You knew my phone was confiscated. You could've tried the landline! Emailed me! Written a letter, hello, Ms. Stationery Queen!"

I sit back in my desk chair, embarrassed and ashamed. She's right. I could've done all of those things. "I'm sorry. I should've tried something else."

"Uh-huh. Put that in your FFFM journal! Maybe you give up when things get hard with people. Ever thought about that?" She laughs a sinister, kind of over-the-top fake laugh, but then she sort of moves on from it. "I'm home sick today. So bored I decided to try to dye my eyelashes." She closes her eyes to try to show me.

"Wow, is that even safe? Could you go blind or something?"

"No. And chill out." She rolls her eyes now, and to be honest, I can't tell that she did anything different to her eyelashes. "Anyway, since you still haven't asked me what happened with the cheating scandal, I'll inform you that they discovered that Pearl was lying, I did not cheat, and now little miss liar needs to serve a week of at-home suspension. And I got my phone back! So there."

"Wow, that's great!" I smile. "I knew you didn't cheat."

"Really?"

"Yes. Of course."

Adelaide glares at me. "So, yeah, I know we're not like real friends-friends, but I sorta thought you cared a little."

My throat tightens; it feels like stacks of staples are sitting on my tonsils. She's right. I should have tried harder to check in.

"You gotta think about this, Len. For the mission, I mean." She pauses. "Take a look at yourself when you're looking at the others, too."

"K." I can barely get the one-syllable not-even-a-word out. I attempt to clear my throat and say more, but before I get a chance to, Adelaide says "Later, Len" and hangs up.

I'm left sitting there holding the phone and feeling like someone literally knocked me over—one of those out-of-the-blue things where you lose your breath and it takes a while to recover and feel right again.

Maybe all along I've been a bad friend, and that's what Adelaide is trying to tell me. It comes back to Rabbi Fink and the whole thing about showing up for people. Maybe I haven't been doing that. Like, at all. The lack of letters to

Maddy last year, not asking Adelaide about the cheating accusation, maybe even Will, too. Who knows for sure?

I guess not with Brenna. She was just a mean little kid; she even admits that herself! But every friendship is different, so every friendship breakup is different. I can't lump them all together.

I go downstairs to the kitchen and carry the big wooden bowl of green grapes out to the front porch. Pontoon traipses behind me. Green grapes are my favorite. Truthfully, I don't know how anyone can eat red grapes when green are clearly superior.

"Tune-Tune." I look down at him and he stands on his back two feet and puts a paw on my knee. "Am I a bad friend?"

He doesn't bark or lick me or anything. He stares, that's it, keeping his paw on my knee.

Clearly I still have a lot to learn.

FriENDship: More Will. Unexpected developments.

I OVERSLEEP AND END UP running so late this morning that I finally take my mom up on her offer to drive me to school.

On the way there, she turns to me and says, "Are you okay? You're so quiet."

"I'm fine, Mom. Just sleepy." I turn away from her a little bit and look out the window. I'm starting to feel crunched with this deadline, like there's still a lot to figure out, and over and over again I feel shocked that Sylvie and I still haven't spoken at all, outside of that one meeting. I can't imagine how I'm just going to start talking to her again, out of the blue.

"Jill's been emailing me, by the way," my mom says,

like she just read my mind. "I've been scanning them but not replying. I'm still furious. She still hasn't apologized. Can you even believe it? And Sylvie hasn't talked to you either, right?"

"No," I say softly, and turn toward the window a little more. "You think you'll ever make up with Jill?"

She hesitates. "I don't know. Jill and I go back a while now. And all friendships have bumps and bruises along the way, but this is probably the line in the sand." She pauses and I wait for her to continue. "I'm not sure I can ever forgive her, and she needs to apologize."

"You've had other fights with Jill?" I ask, sort of ignoring what my mom's saying and just asking what I want to ask.

"A few."

"Are you closer with Jill or Louisa?"

At a stoplight, she turns to look at me, almost surprised that I'm asking all these questions. "They're different friendships. Louisa is my best friend since sixth grade. Jill I met when I was pregnant with you. So it's different phases of life, different experiences, different friendships."

"Yeah, I see."

Every day I seem to find another person who's part of the FFFM without really being part of it.

My mom starts talking and she goes on and on and I can't really focus on what she's saying. I need quiet right now; it's too early in the morning and I have way too much on my mind for this.

Please just stop talking. Please let's have some quiet, I secretly plead inside my head.

"Adelaide's having pretty severe stomach issues, so Lou is taking her to a specialist, but I think it could be that Adelaide is trying to be vegan."

"Uh-huh," I mumble back, unable to pay attention.

All I can think about is the deadline for this mission, how I feel comfier but still not totally comfy with AnRuEleEli—now our official name, which is probably too long and clunky. I wonder if I'm not letting myself feel totally comfy with them. If I'm too focused on Sylvie to even realize that other friendships are worth pursuing. Also, none of that really matters because I still can't room with them for the overnight, anyway.

"I think that would be hard if you suddenly tried to be vegan. Please don't do that," she goes on and on.

"Uh-huh," I say again, no idea whatsoever what she's been talking about.

It feels like the ride takes forever and a day, but we finally get to school and my mom finally stops talking. She leans over and kisses me on the top of my head.

"Bye, Mom. Thanks for the ride."

"Bye, Len. Love you!"

I close the car door and walk into school, my head

spinning from how many words my mom said in such a short amount of time. I honestly have no idea what she was talking about.

I take a deep breath and readjust my backpack straps so they sit at just the right spot.

After social studies, I walk to lunch with Anjali the way we always do, and I'm trying to keep up my end of the conversation. It feels like my body is here but my mind isn't.

"So anyway," she says, and even if someone offered me a million dollars I couldn't tell them what she said before that. "I think if you ask Zora to be your roommate, that'll be great, and also did you hear that a new girl moved in right next door to Elizabeth? I think she's starting school today!"

"Um, no, I don't think so."

"Yeah, and so it would be so super nice of you guys to room with her too, and it could be, like, really fun."

"Yeah, maybe," I say, wanting to end this conversation.

I'm doing the agreeable thing again when what I really want to say is that no way does that sound fun, that it feels like we're like a gloppy mess of three girls forced together when we don't want to be, like we're the few remaining cheese fries glommed onto the takeout container from the diner.

We walk into the cafeteria and pass Sylvie's table and Zora looks up at me and half waves and I wonder why she's still sitting there. We're over a month into school and she was all determined to branch out and make new friends and reinvent herself, but she's still there, with the same people, the way it's always been, just without me there, too.

I guess it's harder to start fresh than she realized.

I'm halfway through my sesame bagel with lox and cream cheese when I look up and see Shai and Will standing at our table.

"Oh, hey," I mutter as soon as I'm done chewing.

"Settle a debate with me and Will," Shai says, and at first I'm not sure totally sure he's talking to me, but then he says, "Eleni, when you and Will had your lemonade stand every year, did you use homemade lemonade or stuff from the grocery store?"

I feel really caught off guard by this question and sort of shocked Shai cares this much about lemonade.

Rumi, Elizabeth, and Anjali look at each other with confused faces, too.

"Ummmm." I try to think. "I'm pretty sure from the grocery store." I look at Will. "Right?"

"Definitely not. Don't you remember how we followed that recipe we found online for the best lemonade ever?" Will bursts out with over-the-top lemonade passion. "Guaranteed to help your lemonade stand *stand* out from all the others? And we cracked up about *stand stand?*"

I look around the table and then back at Will, so confused about what's happening right now. My ears feel like they somehow came unattached from my head and spent the last three days on a beach and are now completely sunburned.

"I can't believe you don't remember this, Len," Will says, his eyes turning sort of sad.

"It didn't seem so believable to me either, that second graders would make their own lemonade," Shai adds.

"Who spends this much time talking about a lemonade stand from four years ago?" Rumi mocks. "You guys are weird."

"Well, we had epic lemonade stands," I add, trying to soften the awkwardness and maybe make Will feel a little better. "Didn't we, Will?"

He smiles a half smile. "They were all right."

We're throwing away our lunch stuff when Rumi taps me on the shoulder. "I think Shai has a crush on you."

I whip around to make sure no one is overhearing this. "No way."

"Yes." She nods. "Just saying."

On the walk to science, I force all thoughts of Shai having a crush on me out of my head. I just can't handle it right now; it feels too big and too weird. I think a little more about AnRuEleEli and realize that Elizabeth's the controlling organizer reporter of the group and Rumi's the blunt one who just says whatever she wants to say, whatever's on her mind. And Anjali's kind of like the peacemaker, all-around-nice-person type, close with everyone, holding it all together.

I don't know what role I play. But then again, I don't even know if I'm totally part of the group. I'm getting closer; I just don't know if I'm there yet. And I have a feeling when I'm really part of the group, I'll know for sure.

FriENDship: Will. Continued.

AFTER SCHOOL, I GO INSIDE and drop my backpack and scoop Pontoon up so we can head to the porch to see if Will comes out.

After the lunch lemonade talk today, I feel more optimistic about the Will part of the mission. And after Rumi's crush comment, I wonder if it'll feel easier to talk to Will if Shai's there or if it'll feel harder and more awkward.

Pontoon and I sit together on the porch for a few minutes and I sip a fruit punch pouch (I have an extra one for Will right next to me, in case he comes outside), and I stare at his house, almost praying that he comes out because this part of the mission suddenly has all this intensity.

Like we're almost there, and now the real talk just needs to happen; it needs to progress. Right this exact minute.

I'm about to give up for the day when I hear his front door slam.

I stay outside with Pontoon and munch on a bag of pistachio nuts, carefully placing the shells in a neat little pile next to me.

Will doesn't see me across the street right away, so I stay here and I watch him play tetherball—the ball wrapping around the pole over and over again. And he hits it with such a rage, such an intensity that I start to wonder if he's okay, or if something happened between the lemonade talk at lunch and right now.

I've almost mustered the courage to go over there and see what's up with him when my phone rings.

FaceTime from Adelaide.

"I'm quitting as your friendship coach. I don't want to be part of the mission, I don't care what happens with it AT ALL and I know you don't think of me as an actual friend but I don't even WANT to be your forced friend anymore," she says, running her words together fast. "It's so one-sided. I guess that's your problem and why you're doing it in the first place. There, I solved it. You can stop now."

She hangs up.

I call her back and she doesn't answer. So I text.

Me: Adelaide, please answer.

No reply.

My stomach feels like sandpaper. I know I need to deal with this but I also need to talk to Will because he's outside and something is clearly wrong.

Plus I can't lose the lemonade-discussion momentum.

I scoop Pontoon up into my arms and walk across the street because I can't waste time waiting for him to smell every little thing on the way.

"Hey, Will," I say when I get there.

"Are you here to talk about Shai?" He keeps hitting the ball as he talks; he doesn't look up at me.

"Huh?" I ask.

"Shai. You." He finally makes eye contact. "Boyfriend-girlfriend or whatever?"

"Huh?" I ask again, my heart pounding. Rumi was right, I guess. But also no—I don't want to be boyfriend and girlfriend with Shai. At least not right now.

"All you can say is *huh?*" He hits the ball hard again and then he stands there staring at me for a few seconds before he goes up to the front step for a sip from his water bottle.

I don't know if I should follow him, but I feel weird just standing here.

A few moments later, I go up to the step too and sit down far away from him so it seems like we still have our space but we're close enough to talk.

"I don't know what you're talking about," I tell Will.

"Okay." He shrugs. "So then why are you here?"

I'm not sure why he's saying it so rudely. Seems like he's mad about something. I kinda thought we had connected earlier.

"I, um, well." I stammer a little and try to collect my thoughts so I can say a coherent sentence next time I open my mouth. "I wanted to talk to you, and see if we, like, could, um, be friends again. And, like, figure out why we stopped being friends."

"Dude. What?" Will laughs, shaking his head at me, and I'm regretting this so so much but I can't quit. "You're the one who forgot we made our own lemonade!"

"I know, and I feel really bad about that. But we used to be good friends," I remind him. "And we still live across the street from each other, and so, yeah, I mean, there's no reason we can't still be friends." I pause. "I don't even know why we stopped."

"Uhhhh. Well, you basically just stopped wanting to ride bikes and stuff," he says. "It's like all of a sudden you thought it was weird for boys and girls to hang out and you were always with Sylvie after school, anyway."

"I was?" I ask, my words catching in my throat.

"Uh, yeah," he says like it's the most obvious thing in the world. "She's your best friend, right?"

I'm about to launch into the whole thing with the

sleepover but I stop myself. "It's not that I didn't want to hang out with you or ride bikes anymore. You also stopped sitting with me on the bus."

He shrugs. "Well, it felt kinda weird, I guess. I don't know." He walks back down to the grass and whips the tetherball around super hard and rageful again. "I didn't think you wanted me to sit with you."

"Oh." I look down at my sneakers. "I'm really sorry. That's not how I felt at all."

He shrugs, picking at a scab on his knee.

"Are you okay?" I ask.

"Not really." He turns to face me, pushing around some rocks on the gravel with the toe of his sneaker. "My dad lost his job because he screamed at someone or something and now my mom is mad and it all stinks." He looks at me for a second and then looks away. "He has to go to anger management classes. He probably should've done that a long time ago."

"I'm sorry about your dad," I say, suddenly remembering times when his dad did get really mad over stuff that seemed kinda small, spilled soda and TV remotes left on the floor, stuff like that. "I know this may be a bit weird to say, but I'm still here for you. We do go back pretty far."

He half smiles and does a one-sided shrug.

"I hope we can start hanging out again," I tell him. "For real. Sorry about the bikes thing. I'll still ride bikes with you. Just tell me when. And the lemonade forgetfulness, too."

"Okay, Leni." He stares at the ground. "I better go in and start homework."

"Yup," I say. "Me too."

When I get back to the porch, I realize that step two is complete. Will and I actually talked. We actually reconnected, over the lemonade stuff and the bikes, and he even opened up to me about his dad, like we're real friends again.

I start drafting the Will complete journal letter in my head.

"Hi, Len," my mom says, suddenly appearing out of nowhere.

"You're home early," I reply.

"Yeah, I'm taking a half day, which isn't really a half day since it's almost five, but oh well. I tried." She smiles. "I'm grilling salmon and asparagus for dinner and I picked up some of that potato salad you love from Holiday Farms."

"Yum! I'm starving." Pontoon hops up onto my lap.

"Good news. Adelaide is improving," my mom says, sitting down on the rocking chair next to me. "Figured I'd update you."

"What?"

She looks at me sideways. "I told you the other day. Adelaide had to miss the last week of school. She was having all these stomach issues and she had to see a specialist. She was almost going to go to the hospital but they think it was related to anxiety because of that cheating accusation."

"You told me this?" I ask.

"Yes." She looks at me, concerned. "In the car."

"Did I seem zoned out?" I ask my mom.

"Maybe a little bit." She tilts her head and studies me for a second. "Leni, sure you're okay?" she asks. "We have a parents meeting coming up to discuss the overnight and I'm not sure you're really up to going."

"What?" I gasp. "Of course I am."

She rolls her lips together. "Len, you just don't seem like yourself."

"Mom. Stop. Right now I just need to call Adelaide."

She shakes her head, confused, and goes back inside.

I pick up my phone and Adelaide doesn't answer the first three tries but finally answers on the fourth.

"I'm sorry," I say. "Please don't retire as my coach. Please don't quit the FFFM."

"Too late. I don't want to help you anymore. You don't really care about me." She pauses. "We're not real friends. I knew that, but then I thought maybe we were, but now I know we're not. I was trying to be nice to help with your mission or whatever because my mom said you were so upset and in the end you didn't really care about me, you just wanted my help."

"Adelaide, I'm so so so sorry. You're right. I should've called you and checked in. And you are a real friend, honestly. One of the only good parts of this whole mission was actually getting to talk to you outside of family plans. It actually did feel like we were becoming real friends. I'm really sorry."

"Forget it, Eleni. I don't want your sorries. Everything is terrible. Bye."

I sit there, frozen again, feeling like I messed up so badly that I'll never ever be able to fix it.

At dinner, I enjoy the grilled salmon and asparagus and of course Holiday Farms's famous potato salad, but it's hard for me to eat. I can only take super small bites and even then my stomach wobbles like a chair with uneven legs.

I won't be able to complete this mission without Adelaide, especially since one big takeaway is that I'm not always the friend people need me to be.

THE NEXT MORNING, MY MOM takes Pontoon out to pee while I pick at the basket of muffins on the kitchen table. She leaves her laptop open and since I'm basically an investigative journalist now, I can't stop myself from oh-so-casually peering at the email she was reading.

Hi Ruthie,

I hear you. Thanks for the help. I think she's just really having trouble connecting to people. I thought encouraging the Leni friendship would help, but I guess not. Going to speak to her therapist again. Maybe NYC life isn't right for her. Maybe it's finally time to consider the suburbs.

Love you, Lou

My mouth hangs open as I stare at the screen.

I was supposed to help Adelaide? Not the other way around? Or maybe we were both supposed to help each other?

I don't know what to make of this.

I feel like we were both set up on some kind of experiment. Some weird—very, very weird—experiment. And the thing is, I don't know if we can ever really talk to our moms about this, because we weren't even supposed to know about it. Thinking about this for too long kind of makes me a little dizzy.

When I get to homeroom that morning, Rumi and Elizabeth are standing around Anjali's desk. I drop my backpack and walk over to them.

I wait for a lull in the conversation and then I say, "Guys, can I ask you something?"

I hadn't planned to do this, but now it's as if there's no other way. I need to bring as many people into this mission as possible. Maybe it's because my actual coach, Adelaide, is out of the picture. Maybe it's because I'm on a real path to understanding myself and I can't stop now. Maybe it's because this overnight is so close the parents are having meetings about it.

I need to figure out how I can be the best version of my friendship self. I need to figure out if I even belong in this group, if they even want me here or they've just been nice because they feel bad for me.

"Uh, yeah," Anjali answers, not looking up. She's doodling suns and stars on her notebook and she's almost covered the whole page. She's such a talented artist, even her doodles look professional. "Ask away."

"Do you guys think I'm a good friend? Like, do I care about people and show up for friends and stuff?" I manage to get the words out and then my throat feels tight.

"Um, what?" Rumi laughs, flipping one of her braids behind her back. "Show up how?"

"Just as like a good friend, I don't know. Never mind. Forget it," I reply, and look toward the front of the room, hoping Mr. Smith comes in soon.

"Is this still because of the Sylvie party?" Anjali finally stops doodling and looks up at me with wide eyes. "Or because of that night at Longport Cones. . . . I told you that wasn't a thing like a million times."

"I mean, no, but maybe. I mean, kind of." I crack up at the awkwardness of this whole thing, but then I get myself together because it does feel sort of good to be discussing it. "I feel like I've had a lot of friendship breakups for someone who isn't even twelve yet!"

"Friendship breakups?" Elizabeth yelps, and the few kids who are in the classroom already turn around.

I ssshhhhh her.

"We can be your therapists," Rumi tells me. Both her parents are psychiatrists, so I guess she does have a bit of experience in that area. "We can help you! This is a safe space."

"Go on, Len," Anjali says, motioning with her hand. "You have stuff you need to say, and Mr. Smith will be here in two minutes."

I look at them and the tears creep into the corners of my eyes like the little droplets that hit the windshield as soon as it starts to rain.

When I finally get myself together enough to speak, I say, "Well, my best friend from camp, Maddy . . ."

They slow-nod, like I should continue.

"Anyway, we were best friends, like inseparable at camp, always together, and then she got into soccer last year, and she tried to encourage me to do it, but obviously I'm not athletic, and then she just sort of ditched me for the sporty girls at camp, and I felt so lonely, which was sad because I love camp." I stop talking for a second and catch my breath. "And then I came home and did the Sylvie party planning and then the whole thing happened with the sleepover. And it just felt like I was losing all these friends."

I look at them, but I can't figure out their expressions.

Is it pity? Sadness? Sympathy? I don't know. Maybe all of it combined.

"Well, you're a good friend to us," Elizabeth replies. "Did you ever think that maybe you just picked the wrong friends in the past? Or that some friendships are only meant to last for a short stretch of time?"

Usually she's the controlling one who just tries to make decisions for the group and force us to be this tight-knit thing, but right now she truly feels like a guru, like a life coach who makes motivational speeches for arenas with thousands of people.

I don't know why I never realized before that she's actually super wise and calming.

Elizabeth continues, her blue eyes staring right at me. "Len, it sounds like you were glued to this Maddy girl and then glued to Sylvie, Paloma, Zora, and Annie, but let's face it—mostly Sylvie." She sniffles. "Maybe that's the thing. You always felt like you had to be glued to one person to, like, show that you were loyal and a good friend, but you can be a great friend and be close to many people!"

"Maybe," I finally answer her. "Thanks so much for talking to me about this, guys."

"Of course!" Anjali smiles. "Len, first of all, you're the only friend I've ever had who happily eats my mom's spicy Indian dinners. I mean, you haven't in a while because you haven't come over in forever, but you used to! In like first grade! That alone is a sign of a good friend."

"That's not fair," Elizabeth answers. "I don't like spicy food! Rumi is used to it because of her Korean heritage. And Len is very kind. But it doesn't make me a bad friend just because I don't like spicy food!"

"Okay," Anjali says, resigned. "I take it back."

But then she makes eyes at me like she stands by what she said and I feel good about that.

Mr. Smith comes in and dings the gong and we start with a quiz game about the states and capitals and it somehow leads to a discussion about diversity and white privilege and it feels good to all be talking as a class and voicing our opinions. I like how Mr. Smith sort of treats us like grown-ups or maybe teenagers and makes us feel older than we actually are and he cares about our thoughts and opinions and viewpoints.

On the walk to lunch, I think about what Elizabeth said about picking the right friends and about how maybe I do attach myself to just one person.

That feels like another piece of the puzzle.

Eventually I'll have all the pieces and the whole thing will come together and make sense.

FriENDship: Will. COMPLETE.
A part of the mission I didn't know I had when this started: Adelaide

AFTER SCHOOL, I HEAD UPSTAIRS to finally write my Will complete letter in my journal.

Dear Will,

I really don't know what my life would like without you across the street. It would definitely be more boring. I never would have had a bike-riding partner or a lemonade-stand partner and you were the best person to have by my side at all the Pine Street block parties. Remember that dance we made up in the bounce house?

I'm sorry I took all that for granted and made you feel like you didn't matter and that we couldn't be friends anymore and that I only wanted to be with Sylvie. That wasn't true.

I'm so glad we talked. I'm here for you. I know struggles with parents can be really hard. I go through that more than anyone really knows. Maybe one day I'll tell you about it for real.

Can't wait to play tetherball and ride bikes again.

Your neighbor and friend, Eleni

I munch on green grapes and try to get up the courage to call Adelaide. I didn't need another thing to feel nervous about and I'm not sure I can handle it. But I'm here, and this is happening, and I have to get myself out of it.

I FaceTime Adelaide and it rings three times and then she finally answers.

"What?" is all she says.

"Hi. Can we talk?" I ask, heart pounding.

"You can do whatever you want. You don't need my permission." She stares at the phone, expressionless.

"Adelaide, you know what I mean." I lean my head back against my pillows and try to stay calm.

"Just go, Eleni. Seriously."

"I'm sorry I didn't reach out about the cheating lie and I'm even sorrier I didn't reach out about the stomach problems and the anxiety," I say.

"Why didn't you reach out? Just be honest." She's not

looking at the phone so all I see is her ceiling fan whir-ring and whirring around and around in circles. I can't tell if it's soothing or making me dizzy.

I hesitate. "You really want me to be honest?" I ask.

"Yes. Eleni. Don't you know by now that I don't say stuff I don't mean?"

"Fair." I swallow a few times and choke back some unexpected tears. "So, basically, I didn't reach out because I'll be honest—"

"Yes. Honesty. We've established that," Adelaide inter-rupts.

I try to stay calm, wanting to defend myself, but also realizing that Adelaide is hurt and I need to focus on that, too. "First of all, I was distracted and too focused on my own stuff, that's a big part of it." I pause. "But also, Adelaide, I didn't think you really saw me as a friend. I mean, the whole thing with the friendship coach and how your mom made you come over that day." I sniffle; tears are coming now and I can't stop them. "I didn't think you really cared about me, so I didn't think you'd really want to hear from me when you were going through a bad time. Like, basically I thought your hanging out with me and talking to me was some annoying task you were forced into and didn't really want to do."

"Well, it was." She finally picks up the phone, and I can see her face and her cheeks are stained red. Her eyes look wet. "At first, anyway. But then it wasn't. And I sort of thought you cared about me, like we were connecting on this cool thing, and I don't know. It felt different than with my other crappy friends here."

"It did?" I ask.

"Yes. That's what I just told you."

"I'm sorry. I hope we can start again. No coach, nothing required. Just regular friends," I say. "Can we do that?"

She stays quiet and I start to wonder what it would feel like if she said no.

"We can do that," she finally answers. "Ground rules are that we need to always check in on each other. And don't assume I don't care about stuff because I sometimes give that impression. I care about a lot of stuff." She sniffles. "And I hate most people, so consider yourself lucky that I like you."

I sniffle too. "I still find it hard to believe that you actually like me."

"Len, that's one of your main problems. No one's gonna like you until you like you. Why are you so mean to yourself?"

My throat prickles and that staples-on-my-tonsils feeling starts to creep in.

"Tell me."

"I don't know," I manage to say.

"Well, start liking yourself more, because you're great. I mean, you're also annoying and spacey and the most innocent creature on the planet, but you're also kind and introspective and thoughtful and optimistic and actually pretty fun to hang with." She pauses. "Sooooo . . . stop being so hard on yourself."

"Okay." I wipe some of the tears away from my eyes. "I will."

"But also finish this dumb mission so you can move on from these losers and find better friends," she demands. "You've been wasting your time with the wrong people. I'm sorry. Sylvie Bank is just not that great."

"You barely know her," I mutter.

"I know enough. Stop wasting your time with people who aren't worth it!" Adelaide yells, and puts down the phone again, and I hear a toilet flush in the background, and then I crack up at the absurdity of this whole thing.

"A few other people have said that to me, too," I tell her.

"See? We're right."

"Okay. I will." I pause. "But my mission has led me to realize that some of the friends on my list may be worth keeping. Will, for example. And Charlotte. Probably Brenna, too, actually. A good Hebrew school friend. Not everyone is a dud."

Adelaide cracks up and throws her head back. "Quote of the year. Not everyone is a dud—Eleni Klarstein." She pauses. "Also, there's one other thing you need to do to make it up to me, kind of like a punishment for your sucky friendship vibes, but it won't be that bad."

"Ummm. Okay . . ." I widen my eyes.

"Come with me to this community service thing at my school. Rise Against Hunger."

"Okay, sure, I'll do whatever it takes! I'm showing up for people FROM NOW ON," I yell, laughing. "Send me all the info."

We laugh together on FaceTime for a bit more and then I realize it's almost five thirty and I need to actually start homework because we're meeting my dad at Bizen for dinner to celebrate him finishing this major project he's been working on for months.

In his words, "Let's celebrate by eating as much sushi as we can eat without getting sick!"

SO THAT'S EXACTLY WHAT WE do. Well, what I do.

I eat so much sushi that my parents literally have to help me up the stairs and put me to bed. My stomach is so full it feels like I'm pregnant with three elephants. It was worth it, though. Sushi is always worth it: spicy tuna rolls and salmon avocado rolls and edamame and a few pieces of fatty tuna too.

For my family, it's impossible to be sad when eating sushi. It is literal happy food. My mom is the best version of herself when she's holding chopsticks at Bizen.

That night, I fall asleep so early, at eight thirty, so I'm wide-eyed at six the next morning and ready to launch into the day. This never happens to me.

I brush my teeth and get dressed and go downstairs to

search for some breakfast. I'm still kind of full from the sushi, but breakfast is the most important meal of the day, so a girl's gotta find something. I settle on a yogurt smoothie and take Pontoon for a walk around the block.

He seems shocked, but pleased, that I'm up so early.

On our way back, I notice Will is outside on his porch, playing a handheld video game. I guess he's an early riser today, too.

"Hey, Will," I say. "You're up early!"

"I could say the same thing for you," he replies, only half looking up from his screen.

I stand there as Pontoon takes a little rest on his front lawn, probably confused why we're not just going home. I turn around, about to head across the street, when Will says, "My parents are screaming at each other again. It's kind of like their morning activity now. I guess it's like how some people work out in the morning?"

I want to make a joke about how they're early risers, too, but I stop myself.

I don't know if I should go up to the porch and sit down, but then I decide not to, because he probably doesn't want me to hear the screaming. So I just stand there on the lawn, and let Pontoon rest, and wait to see if Will says anything more.

"I don't understand the point in fighting about my dad losing his job," Will adds a few moments later. "It's so dumb. Like why make a bad thing even worse?"

"Yeah, that sounds really hard, Will," I add, thinking about how I messed up so much with Adelaide by not being there for her. I want to do the right thing now. I think about telling him about my mom's struggles, but then I realize this moment is about him, not me.

He looks up and shrugs. "It is. I hope he gets a new job soon."

"Me too."

It's quiet for a few seconds and my mind wanders back to the friendship mission and which friends should be kept around and which shouldn't, and the whole thing Elizabeth said about picking the right people.

Will should be kept around. Partially because he's my neighbor and partially because I didn't realize how much our memories meant to me until there weren't any new ones to add on to the pile. All this time, I didn't even know how much I missed the tetherball and the lemonade stands and the bike rides. It's like I forgot how much fun we used to have together. And also, Will needs me. He's going through a hard time and I'm not even sure how long it's been going on.

"I better get ready for school," Will says.

"Yeah, me too." I hesitate. "Sit together on the bus?"

He nods.

My heart feels full and warm and proud.

I get inside and let Pontoon off the leash and my parents don't seem concerned about my early morning walk. They're at the kitchen table, reading news on their phones and sipping steaming mugs of coffee, the way they do every morning.

Will and I are quiet on the bus ride, but it still feels good to sit together.

I look out the window and I think about the FFFM the whole way to school. I think about Adelaide too, and the canasta ladies, and, of course, Will, who is sitting right next to me.

It seems like not so much has changed, but at the same time, everything feels different.

It doesn't make sense at all for both things to be true, but they are.

FriENDship: Maddy. Continued.

CHARLOTTE AND I WRITE BACK and forth every week and I love how we've been so great at keeping up with it.

Hi Charlotte!

Doesn't it feel weird that we used to be so close but we barely remember it and now we'll have a new friendship that was so different from the old one even though we're the same people but also different versions of ourselves?

Wow—this letter got really deep. I have been thinking a lot about friendships. I don't understand how they can change so fast, like with your friend Ainsley and me with Sylvie. Like with you and me it changed because we were really little and you moved, but it's like every friendship goes through major changes out of the blue. I hope I'm making sense.

I am obsessed with this glow-in-the-dark stationery so take it into your closet so you can see it.

xoxoxoxo Eleni

After dinner, Adelaide texts me all the things I need to know before the Rise Against Hunger event.

> **Adelaide:** Do not talk to a girl named Brianna Wythe. She's evil.
> **Adelaide:** If a teacher named Mr. Katzamara stops to talk to you, pretend you don't speak English.
> **Adelaide:** If you get bored, walk to the third floor and check out the art gallery. My painting of a toe is prominently displayed.
> **Adelaide:** Again—avoid Brianna Wythe like the plague. She is an actual plague.

I start cracking up at this rapid-fire string of texts.

> **Adelaide:** The second-floor bathroom is the nicest in the building. Definitely go there if you need to poop. For pee, all bathrooms are fine.

Adelaide is one of those people who don't shy away from talking about bodily functions and it kind of creeped me out when we were little, but now I'm pretty much used to it.

I write back:

K got it. excited! See you Saturday!

As I'm falling asleep that night, I think about the event and what it'll be like to be in Adelaide's fancy New York City private school. And then I think about the mission and remember something and feel sort of dumb that it's taken me this long to put all of this together!

Maddy lives in New York City, too! Not near Adelaide. She lives uptown and Maddy lives way downtown in Tribeca, but still. Maybe this is the excuse I need to reach out to Maddy. I'll say I'm in the city for something and can we meet up for ice cream and maybe I can open the door to talking again, or to at least discussing what happened at camp and what happened with our friendship.

The talking face-to-face thing has really helped and now I actually have a real way to make it happen with Maddy, too.

I toss and turn all night, kind of just waiting for morning, when it'll be an appropriate time to reach out to Maddy. I could email her now at three a.m., but that would probably make it all seem even weirder than it already is.

I pull Pontoon up from the foot of my bed and cuddle with him until I finally fall asleep.

The next morning, I spring out of bed before seven even though I'm so drowsy from a bad night's sleep. I brush my teeth and throw on my comfiest jeans and my favorite faded gray crewneck sweatshirt. I sit down at my desk and draft an email to Maddy.

> Dear Maddy,
>
> Hope sixth grade is going great. I've been thinking a lot about what happened this past summer and realized that maybe things weren't so good even before camp and maybe I wasn't as good of a friend as I could have been.

I delete and start again.

> Dear Maddy,
>
> How are you? Hope sixth grade is going great! I am going to be in NYC on Saturday and wondered if you were free in the afternoon. I miss you and would love to see you! Maybe this is weird since camp was weird and maybe you don't consider me a friend anymore, but.

I delete and start again. Again.

> Dear Maddy,
>
> Hi! How are you? I know things are weird between us but I'm actually going to be in NYC on Saturday and I wondered if we could meet up and

talk. I miss you.

Write back soon. I hope this can work.

Love, Eleni

I run downstairs because even though I woke up so early I'm in danger of missing the bus again because it took me forever to write that three-line email. I grab a granola bar from the pantry and say goodbye to my parents, who are discussing taxes at the kitchen table. I scoop Pontoon up and kiss him on the head and sprint outside.

When I get to the porch, Will is standing right there as if he was about to ring the doorbell.

"Oh! Will! You scared me."

"Sorry." He clenches his teeth. "I wanted to see if you, uh, wanted to walk to the bus together."

He scratches an itch under his ear and doesn't make eye contact with me.

"Oh, yeah. Sure."

I run back inside because I forgot to take my backpack off the hook.

We walk to the bus and it's cooler out than I'd realized. "I kinda wish I'd brought a jacket," I say, because it's the only thing I can think of. I don't know why conversations with Will feel easier when we're outside on his porch, but now that we're walking somewhere together, it feels like there's absolutely nothing to talk about.

"Yeah, I'm freezing," he mutters.

"Why are you still wearing shorts? Why are boys obsessed with shorts?" I ask him. "It can be like the middle of December and you and your friends will wear shorts to school."

"I dunno," he replies. "Shorts are cool?"

He looks up at me and for the first time I notice that he has unusually long eyelashes. I kinda want to bring it up to him but he may be embarrassed. Do boys even want to have long eyelashes? I'm not sure.

"Hello?" I hear Will say.

"Yeah?"

"I just asked you something," he tells me.

"Oh, um, yeah," I stammer. "I got distracted."

I wait for him to ask me the question again but he doesn't, and then he just starts talking about how he wants to join the after-school recreation program and how there shouldn't be a limit on how many kids can participate.

"Yeah, I agree with you."

I feel distracted the whole way to the bus and then the whole ride to school. I keep waffling back and forth between whatever it was that Will tried to ask me and the email to Maddy and if she'll respond.

And I'm also exhausted since I didn't sleep last night.

It's going to be a long day.

FriENDship: Maddy

"I HAD AN IDEA FOR the overnight," Anjali says at lunch, dipping a cucumber into some ranch dressing.

"You should've come to the meeting," I answer, faking exasperation.

"You know I couldn't. Anyway. Can you suggest like a thing where we interview a classmate and then it's like we have to write their biography?"

"Are you serious, Anj?" Rumi blurts. "That sounds like torture."

"It does?" she shrieks.

"Yes!" Rumi rolls her eyes. "No way. Imagine I get stuck with Abe Melman. He's always farting!"

"Eww," Elizabeth screams. "I'm eating! Leftover

meatball sub, too. My favorite."

"Sorry." Rumi shakes her head.

"Actually, Abe is so funny," I say. "He was in my small group. He didn't fart once!"

They all crack up at that, but Elizabeth does make an *ewww* face again.

"Did you want to hear my idea?" Elizabeth asks when she stops chewing.

I nod. "Yes, of course, but again, there was a meeting, people!" I widen my eyes.

"Group journal," she says. "We all write an entry and then they print it for us at the end."

"It's only one day," Rumi chimes in. "Is there time?"

"We'll find time!"

Rumi shakes her head. "Why are you all making this so academic? What about games like get the Oreo from your forehead to your mouth? Stuff like that!"

"Ooh! Yes!" Anjali smiles, looking up from her cucumbers. "That one is good."

After lunch, I check to see if I have an email reply from Maddy and then I notice that I have four texts from Brenna. Even though we're not supposed to have phones in school, we all do, and we all sneak little peeks at them throughout the day when we go to our lockers to switch our books between classes. I try to almost squeeze my whole body into my locker, with the phone resting on the top shelf, so none of the teachers can really see what I'm doing.

I can't just ignore this.

Brenna: Hey

Brenna: We have no school bc of a teacher planning day or something

Brenna: Are you in school today?

Brenna: Did u hear our class is leading a service in November

Me: Hi sorry just saw these texts

Me: I didn't hear that about the service

Brenna: Yeah my mom told me, she heard at some meeting at temple last night

Brenna: You're gonna def need to help me

Brenna: I am sooooo bad at Hebrew

Me: Hahaha kk

Me: I'll help

Me: Don't worry

Brenna: (praying hands emoji)

It's kind of cheesy and I'd never say this out loud, but helping people is honestly one of my favorite things. The fact that Brenna wants my help with Hebrew feels big. The fact that she's texting me again feels even bigger.

Without the FFFM, I would have never talked to her

this year. Maybe I'd have never talked to her again in my whole life.

After school, I sit on the porch, munch on pistachios, and refresh my email again and again and again. What if Maddy never responds? Would I email her again? I honestly don't know.

I refresh and refresh: something about a sale at Kayak & Co pops up, and then an email about a neighborhood pre-Halloween gathering outside of Longport Cones. A little while later, two emails from school about homework policies and absences, and then finally an email from Maddy.

> **Hi Eleni,**
> **I am free Saturday.**
> **What time?**
> **—Maddy**

I write back right away.

> **Hey Maddy,**
> **Can we do 4 p.m. at the little patisserie down the street from your apartment? Remember how I loved the blueberry scones from there? HAHA. I was obsessed.**
> **Let me know.**
> **—Eleni**

FriENDship: Maddy

WE DRIVE INTO THE CITY on Saturday morning for Rise Against Hunger and my stomach churns with nervous excitement the whole way. My dad and Adelaide's dad aren't doing it with us, but my dad is driving us in and he's planning to help Adelaide's dad with all sorts of stuff around their town house. Since my dad is a contractor, people always ask him for help, and I think he loves it. He's one of those people who really like to feel needed. I guess I'm like that, too, with helping Brenna with Hebrew and my idea about my mom helping Rumi's grandma.

My mind wobbles from being excited to see Adelaide and her school and do this project with her to freaking out about this plan with Maddy. I try to envision what it'll be like sitting there, across the table from her, all on my own. What if I freeze and can't talk and my mouth just hangs open the whole time?

It sounds weird, but it could honestly happen.

"I'm so proud of you for being excited about this community service thing," my mom says from the front seat, turning her head around a little to see me. "I think it really means a lot to Adelaide that we're coming."

My mind goes back to that email that I read, where Louisa mentioned encouraging my friendship with Adelaide. I guess she does need me almost as much as I need her, maybe the same, actually.

"Yeah. It sounds really cool."

"And what's the story with meeting Maddy? We'll go after, and dad and I will find something to do while you chat?" my mom asks, and I can tell she's sort of opening the door for me to add additional details.

"Yeah. Sounds good."

We listen to the music for the rest of the ride (Grateful Dead, my dad's favorite) and we don't really talk. Before I realize it, we're outside of Adelaide's school, and she's waiting there for us with her mom.

"Hooray!" Louisa says, pulling my mom and me into a group hug while Adelaide stands on the side, her arms folded across her chest, like she was literally dragged here by the collar of her shirt.

It's kind of strange how Louisa is always so cheery and peppy and Adelaide is usually disgruntled. If you randomly saw them on the street, you'd never guess Adelaide was Louisa's daughter.

The four of us chitchat for a minute and Adelaide reminds me to stay away from Brianna Wythe, for the thousandth time. Maybe Adelaide needs a FFFM too, to sort out her feelings about this girl. And probably the others like Pearl Mosley, too.

We walk inside the building and it sorts of feels like an old castle with these stone walls and intricate archways, like a school from another time, a fairy tale, maybe.

Inside the gym, all of these stations are set up and there's a guy on a stage at the front yelling into a megaphone, counting down until we begin. Upbeat pep-rally music is blasting from the speakers.

"We need to watch a video first," Adelaide explains. "It'll tell you what to do. I like to be a weigher, so people bring us the bags with the beans and the rice and the protein packs and then we weigh them at the end before they get packed in the boxes. If a bag is too light, add more rice, and if it's too heavy, take some rice out."

"Sounds amazing." I nod. "I'll do what you do."

She rolls her eyes at me but then puts an arm over my shoulder. "Oh, Len. You innocent little plum of a creature."

I don't know exactly what she means, but I don't focus on it. I'm too pumped up to make all these meals and I'm grateful for it because it's taking my focus away from my wobbly stomach about seeing Maddy later.

We watch the video and it's exactly like Adelaide explained it. My mom and Louisa go over to the station where they put in the beans and protein packs, and Adelaide and I go to the weigh station like she suggests.

She says hi to a few kids on the way, but it's not like she's rushing to be with her friends, even though this is her school and I'd guess she'd want to be with her classmates.

I start to wonder more about Adelaide than I ever have before. Does she have friends? Does she alienate people? Does she always *show up for people?*

The guy on the stage with the megaphone bangs a huge gong and it reminds me of Mr. Smith and my homeroom, even though this gong is so loud and so big, I bet people across town are able to hear it.

Every ten minutes or so, he announces that we've made another few hundred meals, and we keep going like that. Time flies by! It doesn't even seem like work. I'm not sure if it's the loud peppy music or the fact that I truly feel like I'm making a difference—but the whole experience is empowering and amazing.

I look over at Adelaide, and she's smiling and bopping her head, dancing a little. I've never seen her like this.

Something magical is happening here. Maybe when we step outside our own selves and our own experiences, and look outward to help others, it also really helps us. Kind of like what Rabbi Fink said at Rosh Hashanah services.

I continue on this wave of deep thinking as I measure each bag and add some rice sometimes and take some rice out other times so each bag is the exact right weight. I imagine people receiving these meals and eating them and feeling nourished.

As we get closer to the end of the event, my stomach flip-flops over and over again because this Maddy inter-action is very, very soon.

"So what are you gonna do?" Adelaide asks me. We've hit a lull in this assembly-line process so we're standing at the table, waiting for more bags to weigh. "Just like launch into it, ask questions, go on some kind of intense monologue about how you feel about her?" Adelaide cack-les and then shoots eye daggers at the girls at the table next to us. I wonder if one of them is Brianna Wythe.

"I'm not sure," I answer. "Maybe just sort of take it minute to minute and see how it feels."

"Interesting approach," Adelaide says. "I can't believe you're almost done with this mission."

"Well, sort of." I sigh. "I mean, Sylvie's last and that's the hardest one, so. I don't know. I feel nervous about it. Plus this overnight is coming soon and totally freaking me out."

"Sylvie's a terrible person," Adelaide says. "That's the takeaway for that one."

I laugh. "Noted. Got it."

"Eleni. For real. Don't you see that in so many of these cases, it was like basic misunderstandings, just common drifting apart, things happening—but nothing about YOU." She puts her hands on my shoulders like she's a rabbi offering a blessing. "Some people just aren't good. And aren't worth it. And you need to accept that and move on."

"I hear what you're saying," I reply. "But I don't know. We have history. I don't know if she's a terrible person. I don't want to believe that. Plus, it may be depressing to admit, but I just want things to go back to the way they used to be. I still really, really, really want her to be my best friend again. I don't know if I can go through life without a best friend, without her as my best friend."

She looks at me like I'm a lost cause. "Fine. Whatever. Suit yourself."

We get another round of bags to weigh and soon the event winds down.

"Today! All of you!" the man on the stage shouts into the megaphone. "Have made! Six thousand meals!"

We all cheer and Adelaide and I high-five. "This was the best. Can we make it a tradition that my mom and I come to do this with you every year?" I ask.

"Love a new tradish. Love a new tradish." Adelaide shakes her head, laughing. "Of course we can, Len Len. Of course we can."

After that, we go back to Adelaide's house and her mom orders sushi platters from Sushi Seki and we eat way too much and drink at least ten glasses of sparkling water. It all feels very fancy. Everything about Louisa and Adelaide and James is fancy even though they're not rude or showy about it at all.

Sushi's probably the only food I'm able to eat when I'm nervous and that's because it's so good and my favorite and I always have a stomach for it. But after my sixth piece of spicy scallop roll, I realize I may have overdone it, and the nerves about the Maddy chat set in and I need to sit on the couch and possibly unbutton my jeans.

"Oh, I ate too much," I tell Adelaide, sprawled across her sectional couch with these awesome little silver studs around the edges.

"Give it five minutes. You'll be fine. Want a Hershey's Miniature? That always helps me."

"Really?" I attempt to sit up.

"Really." She gets up to grab the bag.

For some reason she's right. Two Mr. Goodbar miniatures later, I'm feeling much better.

"K, ready to go Len?" my mom asks, zipping up her jacket.

"Good luck." Adelaide ducks her head like she's sending me off on a very secret, very serious spy mission. "Report back."

"Will do, Captain."

She starts laughing and it feels like I've conquered something. The ability to make Adelaide laugh is no small thing.

James thanks my dad for all the help around the house, though it's sort of weird he needs this help since they can pay for whatever they want. Maybe James just wanted someone to hang with, someone to talk to. So he asked for help with household chores so he didn't seem, like, overly desperate for friends.

On the ride downtown, I start to realize that this mission is bigger and broader than I originally realized. It's not just about me and my friendship fails. It's about all friendships, how they change, how they grow, where they start and end and then maybe even start again.

Is it possible to go through life without friends? I don't think so.

Also, there's friendship stuff to observe everywhere. I'm glad I'm starting to pay attention to it.

33

"SO THAT WAS NICE," MY dad says as we drive down-town to meet Maddy. The plan is that my parents will browse in the independent bookstore next to where Maddy and I are meeting, so they'll give me some space but of course I have my phone to text them if I need help or whatever.

"It was lovely," my mom replies. "Lou and Adelaide were so happy we joined them."

"It was amazing! We are definitely making this an every-year tradition," I add, still a little surprised that a community service event could really be that incredible.

"How are you feeling about this Maddy meetup, Len?" my mom asks in her forced, trying-to-be-chill tone.

"Fine."

When she does this, I give her the shortest replies possible. I know it kind of makes her annoyed but I can't seem to stop myself.

We're quiet the rest of the way and my dad turns on the Grateful Dead and my parents sing and bop along to "Truckin'" and I try to imagine them when they were younger, when they met even.

Lake Buel Camp, where I go, and where my mom went, is in the Berkshires, where my dad grew up. And one night when my mom and her friends were counselors, they were out getting ice cream at Bev's and my dad was there with his friends, and they met and kind of fell in love instantly. That's how they tell the story, anyway.

I wonder if my mom worried about the same stuff back then and got all frazzled when she was overwhelmed. I wonder if my dad liked to fix stuff when he was young, if he was always a calming presence for everyone.

We make it downtown and my dad finds a parking space right away. "We need to buy a lottery ticket. Ten lottery tickets," he exclaims. "This never happens. A parking spot right in front of where we're going!"

For Maddy, it's normal to meet a friend at this neighborhood spot, down the street, but for me it's a little weird to be out in public unsupervised. I won't say that out loud, but it's true.

I walk inside and Maddy's already there, at a table in the back, reading a graphic novel.

"Hey, Maddy," I say.

"Oh! Eleni! Hi!" She gets up and pulls down her hoodie and shuffles her weight, her arms folded across her chest at first. But then she reaches out to give me a haphazard kind of hug.

"Did you already get a drink? Or food? Or whatever?" I nervous-laugh. My stomach flip-flops again and again and I have no idea how I'll eat anything right now, but I can't just sit there without anything in front of me.

"Yes. Blueberry scone, of course, and this coffee drink they make me but without the coffee. It's really just vanilla ice cream and caramel and ice in a blender, but it's so good."

"Like a milkshake?" I smile.

"Yeah! I guess so!" I sort of feel like we've broken the tension and it'll all be okay. It's only mid-October but camp feels like it was three hundred years ago. Trying to picture Maddy on her top bunk bed writing letters is hard. Trying to imagine waiting in line to shower and all of us blow-drying our hair on Friday nights also feels hard.

Maybe it was because of the summer I had and how much has changed since then, but it all feels so far away.

"So this is random," Maddy says, half laughing when I sit back down with a blueberry scone and the coffee-not-coffee drink Maddy suggested.

I try to center myself and think soothing thoughts about pens and stationery and journals. I imagine

Pontoon at my feet on the porch.

"Well, um," I start, wanting to be concise and make sense. "So, like. Here's the thing."

Okay, I am clearly failing at the concise thing. Need to recenter. *Pontoon at my feet on the porch. Len's Pens. Pontoon at my feet on the porch. Len's Pens.*

Of all the FFFM items, this one feels the hardest so far. And if this one is hard, I cannot even imagine how hard Sylvie's gonna be. My heart starts pounding. *Pontoon at my feet on the porch. Len's Pens. Pontoon at my feet on the porch. Len's Pens.*

"So basically," I start again, "I felt sad about this past summer, and how we weren't really friends the way we'd been during past summers. And, like, I missed you, but I didn't feel like part of your crew with Wren and Hattie and the soccer girls. And I couldn't find my place in the bunk." I pause and swallow hard. "It made me so sad because I love camp, but then I wondered if it's possible to love it without best friends, people you really want to be around."

Maddy sips her coffee-not-coffee drink through a straw. I think she's waiting for me to continue but I kind of wish she'd just jump in and say something.

"Anyway, I started sort of thinking back on our friendship and maybe it was my fault because you wanted to bring me into the soccer stuff but I'm just not an athlete." I feel like tears are going to pour out of my eyeballs any minute, and then I start nervous-laughing, and so does Maddy. People start turning around to look at us and this whole scene kind of feels like a debacle.

"Not everyone likes sports," Maddy declares like it's some deep, hidden secret even though it's obviously a fact of life.

"I know that," I say. "I mean, I don't know, I just wanted to talk about it, I guess."

"You still could've hung out with us," Maddy adds. "I don't think Wren, Hattie, and I thought of ourselves as *the soccer girls*, like you say." She raises her eyebrows. "We're just, like, normal friends who all play soccer."

"Yeah, I don't know. I just didn't feel so included." I hope that didn't come out like an attack.

Maddy hesitates before talking, but I sense that she's gonna come out with a big revelation. "Len, can I just say something?"

I nod. Uh-oh. Here it comes.

"So, like, I think you were just used to it being the two of us attached, doing everything together every summer," she starts, and it feels like someone is taking a very pointy edge of a pair of scissors and poking it into the pad of my thumb. "And I kinda wanted to branch out a little. It doesn't mean I don't love you or want to be friends. But then, like, as soon as I branched out—you sort of disappeared."

"Because I thought you didn't want me around!" I yell,

and then try to quiet my voice. "You never saved me a seat at Shabbat dinner, and when I tried to come over during the all-camp dance, you sort of just turned your back to me and danced in a circle with Wren and Hattie and them."

She sips her drink again. "I didn't mean to do that. I would never be mean to you on purpose, Eleni."

I want to say that she *was* mean, and she did hurt my feelings even if she didn't mean to, but I wonder if there's a point to that now.

"I know you wouldn't mean to," I reply. "But it's how I felt."

"Honestly I thought you liked hanging out with Lilia and Shir and the new girls."

I shrug. "I mean, they're fine, but." I stop myself. This isn't about them. "I don't need to be attached to you, just the two of us. Maybe I did, but I don't anymore."

"Okay." She shifts on her chair. "Well, I'm glad you emailed me. And I'm glad we're talking."

My throat tightens because I think there was some part of me that wanted Maddy to say she really missed me, and it was all a miscommunication and we could go back to being how we were, always together, not really needing anyone else.

"Just because you're not the center of a group doesn't mean you're not included, Len," she says like that's a statement that should smooth everything over. It only makes me feel worse, though.

"Yeah, um, I know that."

"I know we did talk about soccer a lot and we were kind of obsessed, though." She takes another sip of her drink. I turn around for a second, looking for the bathroom, and I see my mom peering in through the big window. "I get that part of it, too."

"I mean, you did wear your jerseys allllll the time," I say, sort of joking but also sort of not.

She half smiles. "That's true. I have to admit, you might like soccer if you really tried it, though."

I laugh for a second. "I'm really not an athlete and I think I'm okay with that." I pause. "But also I'm glad we talked," I say to Maddy. "I think I have to go now, to get back home, the traffic and everything."

"Yeah, of course." She nods. "I'm really glad you emailed me, Leni. I'm still excited for camp next summer."

"Me too," I say, again not sure if it's true or not. But it's only October. I have lots of time to get excited.

Maddy and I exchange an awkward hug and I collect my things and go to the bathroom and then walk to the door to meet my mom.

On the walk to the car I think I feel fine at first, but then with each step, I feel a heaviness in my chest and my throat and my whole body basically.

It's this overwhelming realization that things are never going to go back to the way they used to be. Not with Maddy and probably not with Sylvie, either.

I guess that's what the canasta ladies said way back when I started the FFFM, that friendships are always ongoing, evolving, changing. They're never going to stay the same, even if we really want them to.

It'll be okay. Of course it will, and maybe some things will even turn out better than they were before, who knows.

But it will never be the same, and with Maddy, and probably Sylvie, too, that's a really hard thing to accept.

34

Hey Charlotte,

Hiiii. I can't believe your grandma wants to go skydiving! Is your mom really scared about it?

This community service Rise Against Hunger thing I did with my friend Adelaide was so amazing. We made 6,000 meals! For real!

What happened with you switching into the higher math group? You never told me. That's super cool that your school has a mathletes team. I think we only have that in high school here.

Anyway, write back soon. xoxoxox

Love, Eleni

I seal the envelope and lick it and place a pretty heart stamp in the corner.

Then I decide to do something I haven't done in forever. I guess the fall has been busy and the whole incident at Longport Cones kind of threw me for a loop. But I want to actually try and make plans with AnRuEleEli. Go beyond sitting with them at lunch and group texting. Make a gesture that shows I'm putting in some effort.

Maybe that's the thing that'll really make me feel like I'm part of the group. That's definitely a major takeaway from the mission. You can't wait for the other person to make all the suggestions and all the plans in a friendship; you need to do it, too.

I group text and see if they want to come over this afternoon for a backyard hang and maybe some s'mores.

Within six minutes of me sending the text, they all respond.

> **Elizabeth:** YES! We're taking my grandma shopping
> but I can be there by three
> **Rumi:** I am free all day! Woo-hoo!
> **Anjali:** Fab! So excited to hang.

I run inside and tell my parents that they're coming over and I swear I can see their hearts pitter-patter inside their shirts.

"That's so wonderful," my mom says, communicating

with my dad by only widening her eyes.

"We'll try to stay out of your way, Len," my dad adds.

It's strange how once you're out of practice, even simple things like making plans with friends feels like a big deal. My mom puts some drop-and-bake cookies in the oven and she makes some of her famous onion dip, and even though we're nearing late October, it's warm enough for us to be outside on the back deck with jackets on and hang out in the backyard.

My parents tell me they're heading upstairs as to not interfere. I kind of want to tell them to calm down. This shouldn't be such a major event.

I wait outside on the porch for them. I know it seems eager, maybe too eager, but truthfully it's always awkward when people arrive and you have to let them in and then you're just sort of standing there in the entryway of your house. So I figure if I meet them outside on the porch, we can go around to the back and sit there and eat our snacks, and it'll be easy.

I'm waiting for them and texting with Brenna at the same time. It's kind of amazing how we're texting friends now when just a few weeks ago, I thought she truly hated me.

Brenna: This was my last week of early morning stapling! Hallelujah!
Me: Lol.

Brenna: My parents are really happy we are friends again btw

Me: Really?

Brenna: Haahaa yeah

Brenna: Cuz you're gonna help with me Hebrew

Brenna: And also they think you'll be a good influence on me

Me: Hahahah ok

Me: Happy to help

Brenna: LOL

I start to type *BrenLen Forever* but it feels overly cheesy and lame, even for me, so I erase it and I leave Brenna's LOL hanging there.

It's an ongoing conversation.

"We're heeeeere," Anjali sings, getting out of the car. Rumi's mom drove them and she waves to me from the front seat, like she knows me so well and is so happy to see me. It feels like next-level friendship, when someone's mom knows you. That's when you're in a new category of friendship.

"Wait until you guys see my snack spread," I tell them. "Follow me to the back. Prepare to be amazed."

"Oooh, can't wait," Rumi and Elizabeth say at the same time, and then start laughing.

Anjali, Rumi, Elizabeth, and I spend the afternoon eating snacks on the deck and lounging on the hammock and talking about pretty much nothing. I pray in my head that the overnight doesn't come up because I don't want room discussion awkwardness. I don't want to have to pretend I'm okay with it when I'm not.

We start out with Anjali telling us how her Indian dance class is entering a competition and they may win a trip to Disney World and then Elizabeth goes on and on about how she really wants to go to acting camp this summer, and she asks us if we think there's a chance she could be discovered by a movie scout somewhere totally random like Natalie Portman in the pizza place.

"Wait, forget that, we have something super important to discuss," Elizabeth interrupts her own train of thought. "Our costumes! The Halloween party is the night before the overnight now, right?" She looks at me. "We need to figure this out."

"Yeah . . . ," I say, tentative, really not wanting to get into who is rooming with who.

"So what are we all gonna be? Please say yes to group costume! Please say yes," she pleads.

"Okay, chill." Rumi rolls her eyes. "I love you, but chill."

Anjali sits up straight. "Okay. Everyone ready to hear my costume idea? I know you'll all love it because you all love this food. . . ." She looks at each of us like she wants us to guess.

"Hot dogs?" I ask.

"Yes, but no," Anjali replies.

"Pizza?" Rumi asks.

Anjali shakes her head.

"Oh! I know! Sushi!" Elizabeth yelps. "I saw that costume online. Yes! Amazing!"

"Yes! What do you guys think? All of us as sushi pieces?" Anjali asks.

My eyes widen. "I mean, of course. You know me and sushi."

"Amazing idea, Anj." Rumi smiles. "I am so in."

We discuss who's going to order the costumes, and how should we wear our hair, and it feels so good to be a part of something. And a part of something I actually want to be a part of! It's not like with Lilia and Shir at camp. I actually want to be with these girls.

After a few more minutes of the costume discussion, Rumi goes back to the whole *who has a crush on Eleni* thing.

"I think they both love you," she says, tapping my knee when we're side by side on the hammock.

I lift my eyebrows and give her a look. "I really don't think so, Rumes."

"That's the first time you've ever called me that," she says. "Yay! I feel like this is an important friendship milestone."

My skin prickles but in a good way; it's an all-over sense that I'm connecting with someone. "Yes, nicknames are a huge deal for me. I totally know what you mean."

There's so much power in that *know what you mean* feeling.

I'm not sure I ever realized it before, but when you get someone, and they get you, and you both share the same opinion, on even the simplest, smallest thing—it's a huge deal, an electric-current-that-zaps-things-into-place friendship moment.

35

Anjali: Isn't it weird all of our parents are at this meeting rn

Elizabeth: Kinda yeah although my dad is home because they were nervous my grandma would need help

Rumi: Ahhh ok

Rumi: Granny McKinley—what a gal

Elizabeth: LOL

Me: What do you think they're talking about @ this meeting

Anjali: IDK but it's weird they haven't asked us to pick roomies yet

Elizabeth: What if the trip is canceled and we don't know yet

Rumi: Why would it be canceled

Rumi: No offense but E you are sooo weird sometimes

Elizabeth: Idk it's possible

Me: Hmmm

Me: I guess anything is possible

Rumi: Oh Leni, with the almost inspirational quotes

Me: Hahahaha that's me 😃

I guess I'm getting more comfortable with them now because I can sort of laugh at myself a little bit. That's not a small thing.

I hang with Pontoon on the couch while my parents are at the meeting. It still feels a little weird to stay home alone. I guess because I just started doing it. But Pontoon and I cuddle under the yellow-and-white blanket my grandma knit before I was even born and we watch *Fuller House* and every few seconds I think I hear the garage door opening.

I get up to get a mini bag of gummy bears and of course that's exactly when my parents walk in. No garage door warning, since they come in through the side door after parking in the driveway.

"How was the meeting?" I ask.

"Very interesting," my dad says, taking off his jacket and hanging it on the hook in the mudroom.

"And?" I ask, following them to the den.

"It was an informational meeting for parents," my

mom adds, all even-toned. "You'll find out everything you need to know at the meeting for students. It's tomorrow, I think."

"You're being weird," I add. "Why can't you just tell me what they said?

"Len." My dad turns around and pulls me into a hug. "It's all good, I promise. Nothing to worry about." He pauses. "But you really need to be in bed. You're going to oversleep again."

At school the next morning, Sylvie, Paloma, and Annie are whispering about something when I walk in and Zora is sitting with her back against her locker, flipping through a notebook.

My stomach is swirling around like the wave pool at a water park. I think this student meeting is happening today and I can't believe I haven't finished the FFFM yet. I've felt the deadline looming for a while, but this meeting totally snuck up on me.

We'll have to pick roommates before I'm ready, before I've talked to Sylvie. Before I have anyone to room with.

"Hey, Len," Zora says as I walk by, on the way to unload my backpack.

"Oh, hey."

"I'm switching my locker, moving after lunch today," she tells me so I stop walking, realizing this is more than a quick hey. "I just really need a change."

I honestly don't really know what's been stopping her. She's the kind of girl everyone would want to be friends with—smart and pretty and outgoing. I bet if you walked up to every single person in the grade and asked them what they thought of Zora Wilson, they'd say she's nice, cool, pretty—basically all the good things.

She's a universally very-well-liked type of person.

"Oh, okay, that's cool." I nod. "I didn't realize we could switch lockers."

She stretches her legs out in front of her. "I asked Ms. Macerny and she said it was okay and assigned me another one."

I put my hands in my pockets, feeling a need to end this conversation and keep walking. "Oh, that's great, then."

Zora stands up and comes closer to me. "I hope you don't think I was part of this whole thing," she whispers. "Like, they're just sort of bad people. I'm glad you're friends with Anjali and them now."

I look around, not knowing what to say and who's around to overhear. The hallway doesn't seem like the best place for this kind of talk.

"You know I wasn't part of it, right?" she asks.

I'm not even sure what it is. I just want to get out of here, out of this conversation, this hallway, this moment. I was feeling fine before school started; I don't want this ickiness on me for the rest of the day.

I'm about to make up some excuse about how I'm late for extra help when we hear the loudspeaker chime and then: "All sixth graders should go to the auditorium before homeroom."

"Wonder what that's about," Zora says.

I swallow hard. "Hmm, yeah, actually, I think it's about the overnight," I say, and then regret it. "Better go unpack."

"Later, Len."

I get to the auditorium and Rumi, Anjali, and Elizabeth are already there in the second row.

"Leni!" Elizabeth calls out. "We saved you a seat!"

She's always the coordinator, but right now, it's especially comforting and reassuring. Having someone save you a seat is at the top of the list of amazing things that can happen to a person.

I sit down at the end of the row and the rest of the grade comes in. Off to the side I see Zora with a group of girls who've always been in our grade but I don't really know them so well. I think a few of them do competitive horseback riding together because they presented about it at an assembly last year.

Zora smiles when we make eye contact; her shoulders look more relaxed. Maybe she's been branching out this whole time, but I really only saw her in the cafeteria and our lockers so I had no idea.

I wonder where she'll sit at lunch today.

I pick at the rough skin on my thumb, unable to focus on what Anjali, Rumi, and Elizabeth are talking about. All around me, conversations are buzzing, and it feels like I'm trapped in a room without any doors or windows and all I want to do is get out into the fresh air.

This is going to be it, the moment they tell us about the trip. They're going to hand out little slips of paper and golf pencils and we're going to have to write down our name and who we want to room with. I just know it; I can picture it.

And everyone's going to lean forward on their chairs and look down the rows and say things like "I'm putting you down" and "Best roomies ever," and they'll high-five, and everyone's going to be set and secure and excited; it'll be an official countdown to the trip.

And then there'll be me. Alone. Stranded.

I'll have to tell the teachers I don't have anyone to room with and they'll say things like, "Don't worry sweetie, we'll figure it out" and "It's okay," but really they'll just feel bad for me, looking at me with their sad teacher eyes and then talking about it to each other in quiet voices in the teachers' lounge.

Ms. Baldour, our principal, comes to the podium. "Hello, students, lovely to see all of you," she says. "I hear from your teachers that sixth grade is off to a wonderful start and I am thrilled." She pauses and then scans her notes. "First of all, our student planning committee has done an amazing job coming up with ideas for the overnight. I am so impressed."

She looks out at the grade and smiles. "But I know there have been many rumors circulating about the sixth-grade overnight: that it's canceled all of a sudden, that it's just a day trip this year, that we're doing it in half-grade groups, and on and on. This happens every year, somehow, no matter how hard we try. It's a big event in a big year and we understand that." She pauses again and clears her throat. "There *have* been changes made to the trip this year, and it's important that you know what they are, and why we made the decisions we made, so we are all on the same page, and we all understand what's happening."

Elizabeth looks down the row at us. "See, canceled, I told you!"

"Shhh." Rumi shakes her head, giving me a *what is wrong with her* look.

Little side whispers and what-is-happening conversations pop up all around us and the teachers try to quiet everyone down.

Ms. Baldour continues. "Our goal at Longport Middle School is to create an environment where everyone is included and respected, where we can learn from one another, appreciate our differences and our similarities, and really expand our social circles. For many of you, you've been in the Longport schools since kindergarten, with the same friends, at the same lunch tables, and that's lovely. We've tried to keep friends together at lockers, but middle school is really a time to branch out, a time to talk to new people, and a time to gain some new perspectives. This is our goal for the overnight, it always has been, and after much discussion, we've realized we've fallen short in recent years. So we are making some changes." She clears her throat again. "This year, bunking arrangements will be assigned, buses will be divided by last name, and we will all go into this with open minds and open hearts."

She ignores the groans and *oh mans* and the suddenly much louder stir of little side conversations. Eventually everyone quiets again.

"Yes, it's still around Halloween and yes, we have moved the party to the gym the night before we leave. You can all dress up, and have fun, and come up with imaginative, wacky costumes. I can't wait to see them." She pauses. "I just want you to all be aware that at Longport Middle School and on this trip especially, our number one goal is to create an environment where not a single sixth grader feels left out." She looks out into the auditorium, kind of scanning all of us, smiling. "If I hear of anyone complaining or making trouble about this, you'll be immediately sent to my office so we can discuss it."

The auditorium is silent. Even Abe Melman and his friends aren't making farting sounds or tapping each other or kicking the seats in front of them.

She continues. "If you have questions or concerns, you can come talk to me or send me an email and I'll do my best to address them." She smiles. "I know this will be a transformative experience for all of you. And before you go: a few of the amazing ideas from our planning committee. Get excited for Create Your Own Jenga, a rubber-band-ball-making contest, Dress Your Teacher Like a Mummy." My heart perks up. Sylvie and my idea. I look over at her, assuming she won't glance in my direction. But she looks at me at the exact same second. My heart is a shade of pink right now. Even with all the bad things with Sylvie, we did make this one thing happen together. Ms. Baldour may have listed more ideas after that, but I was too caught up in this to hear them. "Have a great rest of the day!"

Everyone starts shuffling out and I know I need to get up since I'm on the aisle, but I am frozen stuck in this auditorium seat. It's an overwhelming feeling of relief and defeat at the same time; it's two different spreads—like cream cheese and peanut butter—on two slices of bread about to be smooshed together.

Assigned roommates is pretty much a dream come true for me, and even assigned buses is kind of amazing;

it takes all the stress out of worrying who you're going to sit with.

But now it sort of feels like the FFFM was pointless. A waste of time.

I don't know if I even need to finish it and talk to Sylvie, if I should just listen to what Zora was saying earlier. *They're kind of bad people.* Maybe it's true. I have other friends now, and they're good and kind and fun and they're not my best friends yet but maybe that's okay. Maybe we'll get there.

"I don't even know what to say," Elizabeth announces to us when we get to homeroom. "I'm kind of surprised they did this."

"I know, it's super weird but also, I kind of think it's a good thing," Rumi says. "I mean, it's one overnight. So what if you're with someone you don't like or someone who smells bad or someone who snores, you're not gonna be in the room that much."

"It would be more fun with a friend roommate, of course, but yeah, I guess I see what you're saying," Anjali adds. She looks toward me. "I bet Sylvie is soooo mad."

I shrug. "I don't know. Probably."

"She's definitely mad," Rumi says. "I wonder if she'll come up with some excuse not to go now."

I take that in for a moment; the thought hadn't even occurred to me. I wonder if after all of this, and the planning committee and looking forward to this overnight since sixth grade, Sylvie ends up not even going.

Mr. Smith comes in and we all sit down, and I think to myself, *Of course Sylvie is mad.* And if we were still best friends, the way we used to be, I'd be so mad, too.

So many things have led me to realize that Sylvie is not the person I thought she was, that our friendship wasn't the friendship I thought it was. Of course, this overnight is obviously not the trip I thought it was.

And yeah, that's all true. But I still need to finish the FFFM.

Sure, it started all about getting Sylvie back in time for the overnight, but it grew into way more than that—an exploration of friendship, an exploration of me and who I am as a friend.

I'm almost there, too close to the end of something super important to just abandon the whole thing.

FriENDship: Sylvie

WE'RE THROWING AWAY ALL OF our lunch stuff and
everyone is scrambling back to their seats to be silent in
time for the after-lunch announcements. Any table that's
noisy has to stay after and help the cafeteria staff clean
up, so it behooves (Mr. Smith's word) us to be quiet.

"Hey, Sylvie," I say as we're at the same garbage can,
dumping half-eaten sandwiches into the trash.

I need to speak up. I need to do this.

"Can we talk after school today? We can sit on the
bench in the courtyard and take the late bus or you can
come home with me and we can sit on the porch? My
mom made homemade chocolate chip scones last night.
They're really, really good."

I'm running my words together, talking super fast and coming on too strong. I know I am. I think it's my eagerness to finish the FFFM. Maybe also the confidence that this overnight (and maybe even our friendship) just doesn't really matter anymore, at least not the way it used to.

"Sure. Yeah." She plays with the curls at the end of her ponytail. "I'll come over. The scones will be amazing, I'm sure. Your mom is the best baker I know."

My eyes almost pop out of my head in shock.

"Really? Oh, um, yeah, she definitely is." I swallow hard, as if that's going to get rid of my absolute astonishment and help me to remain calm. "K, cool. So, yeah. So, um, see you at the bus?"

"Or at the lockers. Whatever." She shrugs like this is absolutely no big deal and we make plans to hang out all the time and everything is normal between us and we haven't been silent with each other for almost two months.

I make it back to my table in time for the after-lunch announcements and Rumi makes eyes at me, like she witnessed the whole thing.

I make eyes back that we'll talk after lunch but I'm not sure she understands what I'm saying or not saying, I guess.

The announcements are short today, just something about how we're going to start composting and also about how Pizza Friday is canceled this week because Slices is undergoing some renovations. I'm not sure why they couldn't pick another pizza place, like my favorite, Mozzarella Sticks, for this week.

On the way out of the cafeteria, Rumi comes up beside me.

"I saw you talking to Sylvie," she says, and we link arms.

"Yeah. I want to sort things out between us," I reply.

"She's so mean and horrible, Eleni." Rumi stops right there in the middle of the hallway. "I know you were worried about roommates for the overnight but it's not a thing anymore. Seriously, don't try and become friends with her again. Okay?"

The skin all over my body suddenly tightens and I don't know what to do or how to respond to her. "I didn't say I'm trying to be friends with her again. I've known her since before we were born and it's weird, so I just want to sort of figure it out."

Rumi shakes her head. "Not worth it. But okay."

We're quiet the rest of the way to our classes but we stay arms-linked, and by the time we part ways, we burst out laughing that we walked that way the whole time.

I meet Sylvie at the lockers at the end of the day.

"Ready?" she asks me.

I can feel Paloma and Annie observing the situation

and it makes me shaky, like the time we took the ferry to Connecticut and I was all wobbly getting off of it.

I guess this would be easier if no one else was watching us.

Sylvie and I get onto my bus and then there's the realization that I need to survive this whole ride. I didn't think about that. I imagined Sylvie and me on my porch, eating scones and chatting like the old days, but I didn't think about what would actually happen on the ride to my house because it's not like I can launch into conversation with people all around us, and it also feels weird to just talk about boring, mundane everyday stuff. And then sitting there in silence—that also feels completely awkward.

There's no good solution.

I go to my usual seat and scooch in near the window and then I see Will come in; I think he's about to sit next to me like he's been doing lately. But Sylvie swoops in before he has a chance, and then he's just standing in the aisle. I open my mouth to say something, but no words come out and my jaw is left just dangling wide open.

He's going to think I abandoned him for Sylvie again, like I've learned nothing at all from what he said, but there's no way to explain anything to him right now.

"Will is so weird now," Sylvie whispers as if things are fine between us and it's a totally normal thing to just gossip about someone on the bus together. "Do you notice it?

Shai doesn't want to be friends with him anymore."

My throat tightens. "Shh," I say. I don't want him to overhear.

My mind flashes back to what Rumi was saying, and what Zora was saying. And even Adelaide.

Sylvie Bank is not worth it.

I think they're right. I really think they're all right. I want to cancel this. Maybe the takeaway here is that some people are mean and some friendships aren't meant to continue forever. I thought that was the takeaway with Brenna. But it looks like it's the takeaway with Sylvie instead.

"He can't hear me, Len." Sylvie rolls her eyes like I'm being completely ridiculous.

"He could hear you. We don't know," I whisper, matter-of-fact, and turn away from her a little bit, toward the window.

She shrugs and pulls out her phone and starts scrolling through, ignoring me like I've offended her. We're not even supposed to have phones out on the bus but I guess she doesn't care.

We're quiet most of the way to my house except for occasional snippets of conversation. She pulls up some stuff she's saved on her phone and shows me the new bedding she's getting for her room, and how it's going to be a total upgrade and redesign because her room is so babyish and there's no way it could stay like that now that she's in middle school and definitely, definitely not for high school.

"Are you redoing your room?" she asks me. "Do you still have the pineapples all over?"

Okay, it hasn't been *that* long since she's been in my room.

"I don't know. I guess I'll redo it eventually," I tell her. "I still like the pineapples."

She nods like she was expecting me to say that.

We're quiet the rest of the ride and then we get off the bus. Will follows behind us.

"He's honestly just so weird now," Sylvie hisses, repeating herself from before, and I shh her again.

As soon as we make it onto the porch, my phone starts buzzing from Adelaide FaceTiming.

"Hey. I can't talk," I answer quickly and run my words together.

"Why? What are you doing? Smooching Will?" She cackles, and I really regret answering this call.

"What?" Sylvie stops like she's just seen an explosion.

"Adelaide, I really gotta go."

"Wait. Who's there?" she asks, and then Sylvie snatches the phone away from me.

"Oh, hey!" Sylvie says. "I remember you! You live in the city, right?"

I can't see what facial expression Adelaide is making

since Sylvie is holding the phone, but Adelaide is silent for what feels like three thousand years and then Sylvie hands it back to me.

Adelaide eye-bulges at me but stays silent and then she bangs her head on her desk and hangs up the phone.

"Well, that was *strange*," Sylvie says, dragging out the word. She plops herself down on one of the rocking chairs on the porch. "Where's Tuney Tune-Tunes?"

My heart swells when she says that. Sylvie knows me. She knows the nickname I call my dog. She knows about my pineapple room. She knows my mom is an amazing baker. No matter what happens between us—she'll still know me. We have history. We're connected.

"Len?" she asks. "Hello? Are you there?"

"Oh, um, yeah." I laugh. "Tuney Tune-Tunes is inside. I'll go get him. You want a snack?"

"Um, yeah." She widens her eyes. "The scones."

"Oh, right."

I go inside and feel my brain swirling around and around and around. On the one hand, Sylvie really knows me. She even remembered Adelaide. On the other hand, she's mean and she didn't invite me to her sleepover, and she's rude about Will.

I'm not sure how any of this fits together.

I go inside and grab the scones and two mini cans of Sprite.

I make it back out to the porch and Sylvie's sitting there

with her feet up on the ottoman FaceTiming Paloma.

"Yeah, I don't know. Will is definitely so weird."

"Yeah, very," Paloma answers. "Go do whatever you're doing, hang with Eleni and stuff. I need to go."

"Fine. Bye." Sylvie tries to put on this fake-mad persona and it's weird.

"Fine. Bye," Paloma repeats.

"She's so annoying sometimes," Sylvie says to me as soon as I put the scones down. She says it as if things are normal between us, and that's when it hits me. Sylvie will gossip about anyone and everyone, no matter where or when or who she is talking to. It's like it really makes no difference at all to her.

"Why is she annoying?" I ask.

"She's just so demanding and in charge, like she runs everything we do." Sylvie takes a bite of scone and chews slowly. "I barely get a say."

I see what's happening here. Sylvie likes to be the boss, and I think Paloma does too and Sylvie isn't a fan of that.

"Oh, yeah, I guess I can see what you mean." I bite into a scone too and suddenly feel like I've said too much.

"Eleni, no offense, but you really don't know Paloma like I do." She shrugs like she didn't just say the meanest thing in the world.

"Huh?" I ask. "I've known her as long as you have."

"Len." She lowers her eyes and half glares at me. "You

know it's not the same. You're not friends with her like that. Don't make this weird."

Okay. Enough is enough.

"Sylvie, listen," I start, and then hesitate. "Okay, so I invited you here to talk about the whole sleepover thing." I pause again. "What I'm trying to say is that I thought that since I helped plan the party I should've at least gotten an invite to the sleepover after. To be honest, I felt suuuuuper bad after that, really, really bad." I lean back in my chair. "I needed you to know that."

I surprise myself but also feel kind of proud my bluntness.

"Oh my goodness, Leni!" Sylvie shouts, in a half angry, half jokily exasperated way. "It was so not a big deal. We weren't close all summer. It wasn't like we weren't friends at all anymore because I didn't invite you to one sleepover! And then you just ignored me since then! Didn't say one word! You changed lunch tables! Your mom stopped talking to my mom, even. And now you're BFFs with Rumi, Elizabeth, and Anjali? I mean. Come on, Len. We've been friends since before we were even born!"

I sit up straighter, thinking she's almost done and that I can jump in, but she keeps going, barely taking a breath.

She shakes her head. "I can't deal with this. You're so sensitive. Whatever. I'm sorry." She pauses. "I got super close with Paloma and Annie over the summer. You were away. I mean, it's just the reality and I didn't want it to be awkward at the sleepover since you didn't know any of our jokes and any of the stuff we did over the summer. You would have felt so out of it the whole time and it would have been so weird. But honestly, I didn't expect this to be the end of the entire world."

Pontoon hops up onto my lap. Petting his silky shih tzu fur calms me down the tiniest bit.

"All I'm saying—"

Sylvie interrupts me. "Here's the thing. You need to decide who you want to be friends with. Me, Paloma, and Annie—Zora has totally ditched us but it's fine because she never wanted to hang out anymore anyway—or Anjali, Rumi, and Elizabeth. We're two separate groups. You're always wishy-washy. In and out. You can't, like, commit to friends, Eleni."

I adjust myself on the rocking chair—anger creeps up behind my eyeballs, all over my forehead, spreading to my ears.

She keeps talking. "Maybe that's why you're always getting your feelings hurt. Because, like, you need one friend who is attached to you and has no other friends, and at the same time, you also need a million friends. You need to be part of every group and also have one person devoted to you. It's too much. That's not how it works. Pick a group and be a part of it."

Will is playing tetherball across the street and he

doesn't seem to ever glance over here or pay attention to us. I guess it's far enough away that he can't hear us anyway and watching two girls on a porch isn't all that interesting.

"Hello? Eleni?" She looks at me like a cactus is growing out of my head.

I sit up as straight as possible. "Sylvie, no. None of that is okay," I say forcefully, almost yelling. "I don't need to pick one group. I don't need to just get over what happened with the sleepover." I look right into her eyes. "What you did was mean, heartless, uncaring. Definitely not something a best friend for life does. And it's not just that. You're mean about Will! You're even mean about Paloma, your new best friend. There's a reason Zora ditched you guys—you made her feel left out, too!"

She opens her mouth to speak, but this is my time to keep talking.

"I wanted to figure out what I did sooo wrong for you to just leave me out of a sleepover that I HELPED PLAN and I wanted soooo badly for you to be my best friend again. But guess what? Now I don't. You're not a nice person. And I've actually found other good, kind friends. Anjali, Rumi, and Elizabeth are nice to me! And I like them. And I feel included with them. I need to face the reality that you're just not the friend I thought you were. You're not the person I thought you were."

She sits there with her feet up, staring off into the distance, not looking at me or even responding.

"I honestly can't even believe this," she scoffs. "You're so weird, Eleni." She rolls her eyes and turns away from me. "I feel like you're my sister so I can say that."

"It's time for you to go." I get up and take the plate into the kitchen. Pontoon follows behind me and tries to lick my ankle as I walk inside. Lucky for Sylvie she lives three blocks away and can just walk home. Or she can call her mom. Either way I just want her to leave.

I come back outside and she's texting.

I shuffle my feet on the porch, nervous bubble-wrap bubbles popping inside my stomach. "Sylvie, do you need to call your mom to pick you up?"

She stands up in a huff and picks up her backpack. "Eleni, I'm obviously fine to walk home alone. See you in school."

"See you in school," I reply.

I watch her walk down the few steps and across my driveway and then turn to go toward to her house.

I'm not sure that's how I expected things to go. Pretty sure it's not at all how I expected it to go. But I stood up for myself. I wasn't my usual agreeable Eleni. And I'm proud of that. I really am.

"Yo." Adelaide answers my FaceTime after the first ring.

"Mission complete!" I yell, and then I remember I'm

outside. Will turns around abruptly and stares at me.

"You okay?" he shouts from across the street.

"Yeah. Sorry! Fine!" I shout back.

"Who are you talking to? What is happening?" She puts the phone down so all I see is her ceiling fan for the millionth time.

I take a deep breath. "I finished the FFFM. Sylvie came over today and we talked and guess what?"

"What?" She grumbles out a reply. "Sleeping. Still sort of sleeping. . . ."

"Okay, fine. Just call me back when you wake up."

She jolts upward and pulls the phone to her nose. "Sorry. I'm awake. Talk to me."

"So yeah. I don't want to be friends with Sylvie anymore," I explain. "We talked and it—"

"That loser. She was mean to you?" Adelaide interrupts, her eyes wide like she's really trying to listen and take in everything I'm saying.

I put my feet up on the wicker ottoman. "She kind of just talked for a while and didn't really make sense, but the thing is—I realized something. I don't really want to be her friend anymore."

"Are you just saying that because it's what I want to hear?" Adelaide pulls the phone to her eyeball. "Be honest."

"Honestly, no. I don't like her. She's not so nice, she's mean about Will, mean about Rumi, Elizabeth, and Anjali even though they were kind of her friends . . . I just don't really like her these days."

"Go back to the part about Will," Adelaide says. "Go deeper."

"Huh?" I crack up.

"You love Will. Just admit it. Mazel tov on finishing your friendship mission, but now you may need a love mission."

"Stop!" I giggle, remembering that Will is across the street, but pretty confident he can't hear anything now since his dad just started mowing the lawn.

"Fine. Whatever. Suit yourself." She pauses. "Can I go back to my nap now?"

"Sure."

"So are you going to write up some analysis or something about the FFFM and your findings and submit it to some psychology journal or the *New York Times*?"

I laugh again. "I've jotted down notes. I may write more about it in a journal, though. I ordered a new one from this fancy stationery website a few days ago. It should be coming soon."

"Of course you did." Adelaide rolls her eyes. "Okay, talk later. Back to nappies."

"Bye. Sleep tight."

"Okay, Mom." She cackles again but then blows a kiss to the screen.

I hang up and put the phone on our little porch table.

I sigh with the relief you feel after a dentist appointment, after a math test, after having to tell your parents
you got in trouble but then they say it's okay.

It's the kind of relief that makes you feel you can con-
quer the world.

37

"I CAN'T BELIEVE YOU DIDN'T tell me about the changes to the overnight," I say to my parents at dinner. My mom made spaghetti with vodka sauce and fresh mozzarella, garlic bread, and a Caesar salad.

"They told us to wait," my dad says, scooping some pasta onto his plate. "We follow directions."

"Sometimes." My mom smiles like we're all in on a joke. "Jill is furious, of course. She's acting like Sylvie will be paired up with someone who causes trouble. . . . She made a whole scene with Ms. Baldour at the meeting."

"Not surprising," my dad adds. He turns to me. "How do you feel about it, Len?"

I finish chewing. "Good." I hesitate and wonder if I should tell them about the FFFM but decide not to.

Some things are better kept close, not shared with a million people.

"I'm not sure Jill's the kind of person I always thought she was," my mom adds after a few moments of quiet eating. "It's disappointing, but I'm working on getting better at handling disappointment."

I startle when she says that, shocked. It's rare for my mom to admit her faults and even rarer to admit she's working on fixing them.

It fills me with a sense of hope I've never had before, really. When you're a kid, you can't see your parents as real people with struggles and fears and flaws and frustrations. But they are real people and they go through stuff, too.

But you also can't imagine them ever changing.

I'm still not sure I can imagine my mom ever changing, but I'm open to the possibility.

We finish dinner and there's still a teeny tiny lingering feeling in the back of my brain that the FFFM was kind of pointless. If the whole thing was to get Sylvie back and have the overnight we always dreamed of, and then none of that happened, did I totally fail?

I go upstairs to my room and write my goodbye letter to Sylvie. But first I need to draft some notes, some takeaways, to prove to myself that even if the initial goal wasn't achieved, I obviously learned stuff along the way.

Top Ten Takeaways from the Eleni Klarstein
Friendship Fact-Finding Mission

- Be there for people when they need you
- Make an effort with friends. It can't be one-sided.
- Not all friendships last forever and that's okay
- Friendships change over time and that's also okay
- Don't be afraid to talk to people and be a little vulnerable
- Keep an open mind when it comes to branching out and making new friends
- In life and friendships, there will be bumps and bruises and twists and turns you won't expect
- Sometimes people are going through things you can't understand
- You can't control other people's emotions and how they react to things (this applies more to Mom, but to friends, too)
- If you go out for a special sushi dinner, always get one piece of fatty tuna and make sure the other people you're with do, too. That makes it a real celebration.

Dear Sylvie,

I have to admit, I never expected sixth grade to be like this. I never expected our friendship to be like this. I'm really sad about it. I also have to admit that I don't want to be best friends anymore. I think you're kind of mean and you don't really take the time to think about how what you do affects others, especially your friends.

I'm glad we talked—we'll always have a connection; we'll always have shared memories and history. We'll always know stuff about each other without even realizing or remembering that we know it.

But I'm okay to say goodbye to what we had. For now, anyway.

I don't think I've failed on this mission. In some ways, I succeeded more than I ever expected to.

I learned what I needed to learn, even things I didn't expect to learn. It didn't turn out the way I hoped but I'm fine with that.

And best of all, I feel okay now. Maybe even good. Kind of.

Love, Eleni

RUMI, ELIZABETH, AND I GO over to Anjali's house before the sixth-grade Halloween party.

The moms gab in the corner while Anjali, Elizabeth, Rumi, and I get ready upstairs in Anjali's room.

Her whole house is decorated with Indian art and it smells like the most delicious combination of spices you've ever smelled in your life—spicy and sweet at the same time.

"I am so excited for this party," Rumi says. "And also I am shocked my parents are letting me go."

"Really?" I ask.

"Yeah, they are so strict and don't want me socializing with boys at all. They didn't even let me go to Shai's party last year!" Rumi admires herself in the full-length mirror behind Anjali's closet door.

I feel a little bad that I don't remember that; I guess I didn't talk to Rumi much last year, though.

"Even though this is a school thing. It's different, right?" I ask, trying out one of the new lip glosses I got at CVS the other day. "How did you convince them?"

"I said the whole grade is going; I'll be with you guys the whole time." She spins around, showing off her piece of tuna sushi. "Plus they're letting me go on the overnight so I guess this isn't such a big deal."

"Yeah." I look at the hot-pink clock on Anjali's night table. "K, guys, come on. We can't be late."

Everyone laughs and I look at each of them for a second and exhale a tiny sigh of relief and gratitude and happiness. It's like a triple-swirl ice cream cone of a sigh because right now, I feel like I am where I am supposed to be.

I mean, duh, it's Halloween and I'm dressed like a piece of salmon sushi about to go to a Halloween party, so yeah, I am where I'm supposed to be, literally.

But in all the other ways, too. I really feel like I am where I am supposed to be.

The moms are still gabbing in a corner of Anjali's living room when we make it downstairs and tell them we need to go.

"Okay, file into the car, girls," Anjali's mom, Chummu, calls out. "Party time!"

I look back at my mom for a second and I notice there's

a bit of calm in her smile, peace and relaxation in there, too. I guess she's proof that people can and do change— sometimes, at least. Even the tiniest bit at a time.

I guess when they want to change, they can.

We make it to school and hop out of the car and run into the gym. It's too chilly to linger outside for too long.

"You guys look awesome," Zora says as soon as we get inside.

"OMG, Zora!" I yelp. "I used to love that show. You look so great!"

She's dressed in a kids' *Elena of Avalor* costume and she looks pretty amazing. "I refused to do the group costume thing. Kid character in an ironic way, people! I did it on my own and I'm obsessed. I may do a variation of this costume every year for the rest of my life."

"Yeah, you really look amazing." Anjali smiles.

"I love that idea," Elizabeth adds.

I scan the gym and finally find Sylvie off to the side with Annie's arms around her. I get a little closer and see that she's crying. They did end up doing a rainbow but only red, orange, and yellow and so it doesn't really look like much.

Shai and a few other boys come over to talk to Elizabeth, Rumi, and me, and then I break off a little from the group when I see Will sitting alone.

"Hey, Will," I say, walking over and getting closer to him. I sit on one of the steps of the stage.

"Oh, hey. I didn't see you." He shrugs. "Cool costume!"

"Thanks." I smile. "You okay?"

"Yeah." He replies über fast, which makes me think he doesn't really want to talk about it.

"That's good."

We sit there silently for a moment with all of the party noise around us, and I'm about to stand up and walk to the stage since it's almost time to make the introduction when Will says, "Hey, wanna see something cool?"

I nod. "Sure."

My heart pitter-patters a little even though it's just Will and he's just showing me something on his phone.

"Check this out," Will says, showing me a picture of an ordinary-looking basketball hoop; it doesn't really look like anything special. "It's so awesome; I need to convince my dad to get it for me." He pauses. "I guess I'll wait till he has a job. But isn't it awesome?"

"It looks really cool." I try to pretend to be excited.

"Want to come over and play tetherball one day this week?" he asks.

"Yeah, sure." I smile.

"K. Cool."

After that, the DJ starts blasting "Monster Mash." Anjali grabs my hand and we run onto the dance floor to join Rumi and Elizabeth.

We're dancing and chatting in a circle when I feel my phone vibrating. I wasn't even sure I'd have cell service here. I only brought it to take photos.

"Hey!" Adelaide yells through the screen. I can't see much because it's dark out. "I'm on my stoop, giving out candy! I wanted to see how your night is going."

"Going great," I yell back. It's so loud in here that I walk to the edge of the gym and into the hallway a little, where it's a tiny bit quieter. I say, "Adelaide, I just wanted to thank you for all of your help."

"Oh, LenBurger, don't out cheese your already cheese-tastic self," she yells, and I see her throw a few giant jawbreakers in some kids' bags.

"I mean it, really. You were there for me when I was all alone." I turn around to make sure no one is coming up behind me, eavesdropping.

"CHEESE ALERT," Adelaide yells again. I know she has trouble talking about feelings and I'm only making her uncomfortable, but still. I need to say what I need to say.

"I'll stop in one second," I tell her. "Can I say one last thing?"

"Yes. But I won't promise to listen," she replies, quieter now. The crowd on her street seems to have dissipated a bit.

"Fine. I'll say it fast." I roll my eyes.

"Just go! Spill it!"

"The most important finding of my mission was realizing what a good friend you are," I say as fast as possible, bracing for another scream of how cheesy I am.

"Thanks, Leni." She smiles and I can see her whole face, not just an eyeball or one of her teeth or the tippy top of her forehead. "I obviously didn't embark on a mission, but I kind of feel the same way."

"CHEESY!" I yell, and stick my tongue out at her.

"Hanging up now. Bye."

She's gone before I have a chance to say anything else and I head back inside to the party.

When I started the FFFM, I never could have imagined this is how it would turn out.

I guess that's the final piece of the puzzle, though, kind of. Most things don't turn out the way you expect them to.

And that's probably the very best part.

THE NEXT MORNING, OUR PARENTS drop us off at school an hour before we usually get there. It's dark and there's a chill in the air like winter is almost here; there's an angry-seeming wind that slaps your cheeks a little, making them go numb.

"You ready for this overnight?" my dad asks, getting my pink-and-white personalized striped duffel out of the trunk. "Seems like you've been waiting for this forever."

"Yeah, I guess." I smile. I pull my jean jacket closed and fasten a few of the buttons. I never expected I'd actually wear this, but it's awesome and I love it and who cares if Sylvie has the same one? I'm the person who found them in the first place! "Actually, I think I am."

I hug my parents goodbye and walk toward the buses.

I find the one that says I–K and I go in and sit down near the middle. I'm one of the first ones here, but I feel okay with it, calm even. None of my friends have a last name in my letter group, but that's good in a way. Whoever sits with me is someone new and unexpected. No pressure to sit with a friend or former friend.

It's all open and spread out in front of me, endless possibilities.

I stare out the bus window at all the groups of parents chatting together, and the kids getting out of their cars, lugging bags over their shoulders. I watch the teachers with clipboards, wearing comfy clothes we'd never see them in at school.

Little by little, more classmates get on the bus and shuffle to find seats, walking to the back and then the middle and then sometimes settling at the front, shifting around for what feels like forever until they're in the right spot.

"Hey, can I sit with you?"

I look up, caught off guard at first. And then I smile and move closer to the window so there's more room in the seat.

"Of course," I say.

ACKNOWLEDGMENTS

Infinite thank-yous to Dave, Aleah, Hazel, and Kibbitz for supporting me, believing in me, and loving me, even when I am not the most lovable.

Aleah, thank you for reading multiple drafts of this book and offering such incredible, thoughtful, constructive feedback. How lucky am I that I have such a brilliant tween editor living with me?

Alyssa Eisner Henkin, thank you for the endless support and guidance and for being by my side on this publishing journey.

Maria Barbo, thank you for suggesting this idea, and for helping me make it the best it could be. Your gentle, careful, insightful feedback inspires me to work harder and dig deeper. I am forever grateful that we get to work together.

Katherine Tegen, Sara Schonfeld, Jon Howard, Gweneth Morton, Jessica White, Molly Fehr, Amy Ryan, Kristen Eckhardt, Vaishali Nayak, and Lena Reilly—thank you for all of your hard work and dedication at every step of the process. I feel lucky every single day that I am a part of the HarperCollins/Katherine Tegen Books family.

Katherine Kuehne, thank you for the outstanding jacket art. I loved it from the moment I saw it.

Caroline Hickey and Lisa Graff, my writing buddies since The New School and writing dates in the "dungeon," I am endlessly grateful for our friendship. Amazing writers and amazing friends—what a winning combination!

Rosenbergs and Greenwalds, thanks for showing interest in my writing and buying my books. I am grateful!

To my friends throughout the years from Stratfield to Wheatley, Eisner to Binghamton, The New School to new motherhood in Brooklyn and finally to the Upper East Side, and those friends who don't fit into a category at all: thank you for the love and laughs, the ups and downs, the connections, heart-to-hearts, pillow talk, endless texts, and all the times you made me feel a little less alone. Friendship can be a bumpy ride, and it's not always happy, but I've come to realize that's okay, and that analyzing these relationships is one of my favorite things to do.

Make it a mission to read
The Friendship List! Series,
also by Lisa Greenwald!

Start reading 11 BEFORE 12!

ONE

"KAYLAN!" RYAN POUNDS ON MY door. "You overslept! School starts today! You're already late!"

I run to beat him over the head with my pillow, but I'm too slow. "Ryan," I shout down the hall. "You're a jerk! Karma's a thing, you know. Bad things will happen to you if you're not nice to me."

After five deep breaths, I call Ari.

"You want to go to the pool?" I ask her as soon as she answers.

She replies in her sleepy voice, "Kay, look at the clock."

I flip over onto my side, and glance toward my night table.

8:37.

"Okay," I reply. "I'll admit: I thought it was later. At least nine." I pause a second. "Sorry. Did I wake you?"

Ari sighs. "I'm still in bed, but you didn't wake me."

"Agita Day," I tell her. "August first, red-alert agita levels. I'm freaking out over here."

August 1 signals the end of summer, even though you still have almost a month left. August 1 means school is starting really soon, even though it's still twenty-nine days away.

"Oh, Kaylan." She laughs. "Take a few deep breaths. I'll get my bathing suit on and be at your house in an hour. I already have my pool bag packed because I had a feeling you'd be stressing."

"Perfect." I sigh with relief. "Come as soon as possible! But definitely by nine thirty-seven, okay? You said an hour."

"Okay. I'm up. And you're never going to believe this," she says, half distracted. "I'm getting new across-the-street neighbors."

"Really?" I finally get out of bed and grab my purple one-piece from my dresser drawer. "Describe."

She pauses a second, and I'm not totally sure she heard me. "They're moving the couch in right now," she explains. "I can't tell how many kids there are, but there's one who looks like he's our age."

"A boy?" I squeal.

"Yeah, he's playing basketball right now." She stops talking. "Oops, he just hit one of the movers in the head with the ball."

"Tell me more," I say, dabbing sunscreen dots all over my face. They say it takes at least a half hour for it to really absorb into the skin, and my fair Irish complexion needs all the protection it can get.

I only take after my Italian ancestors in the agita department, I guess.

"He went inside," she explains. "I think he got in trouble. I saw a woman, probably his mom, shaking her hands at him."

"Oops." I step into my bathing suit, holding the phone in the crook of my neck.

"Oh wait, now they're back outside. Taking a family photo in front of the house." She pauses. "He has a little sister. I think they're biracial. White mom. Black dad."

"Interesting," I say. "Maybe his sister is Gemma's age!"

"Maybe . . ." I can tell she's still staring out the window at them, only half listening to me.

"By the way, Ryan is insisting that red X thing is true. You haven't heard about that, right?" I ask.

"Kaylan!" she snaps in a jokey way. "No! He's totally messing with you. Okay, go get your pool bag ready, eat breakfast, and I'll be there as soon as I can."

I grab my backpack and throw in my sunscreen, a change of clothes, and the summer reading book I haven't finished yet. I'm having a hard time getting into *My Brother Sam Is Dead*, although from what I've read, it makes my life seem pretty easy.

I hear Ari's instructions in my head as I get ready, and I already feel calmer. Her soft voice—she's never really flustered by anything.

I stare at my watch again. 9:35. I wait for Ari on the front steps. I'm trying to stay as far away from my brother as possible. Ari still has two minutes, but I wish she was here already.

I stand up and look for her, but she's nowhere in sight. She is so going to be late. On Agita Day.

I learned the word *agita* from my mom. She's part Italian and she learned it from her grandmother, who was 100 percent Italian and apparently said it all the time. It basically means anxiety, stress, heartburn, aggravation—stuff like that.

I don't know what my great-grandma's agita was about, but mine is pretty clear.

Starting middle school.

A few minutes later, I spot Ari at the end of the block, and I walk down the driveway to meet her. She strolls toward me, hair up in a bun, with her favorite heart sunglasses on. Her pink-and-white-striped tote hangs over her shoulder like it's the lightest thing in the world.

"I brought you an extra hair tie," she says, showing me her wrist. "Since you always forget."

"Thanks," I say. "Let's go in so I can grab my stuff. I've had the worst morning."

"What happened?" she asks, after a sip from her water bottle.

I look around for my brother. "I can't even talk about it. Ryan and I got into a huge fight last night. I dumped a bowl of cereal on his head, that's how bad it got. Right as his friend Tyler walked in the door."

"Wow," Ari says.

When we get inside, Ari heads straight to the den and sits down in the brown recliner. It used to be my dad's favorite, before he moved out. I think about him every time I see the chair. I should be over it by now.

He doesn't miss the recliner. He doesn't miss us.

He hardly even calls.

"I've been thinking," Ari says, slipping off her flip-flops and putting her feet up on the ottoman. "I'm gonna go by Arianna when school starts."

My heart pounds when she says this, like more announcements and confessions are coming, like she's going to tell me stuff I don't want to hear. I pick at the mosquito bite on my cheek and try to listen.

She looks at me crooked and comes to join me on the couch. Ari, or I guess I should say *Arianna*, sits up straight, cross-legged, facing me. "Ya know, because, like, it's a new school. I should have a new name. Sound more mature. Sophisticated. That kind of thing."

I nod, but all I can think about is that I need a thing like that. I need to do something big, something to change myself before middle school. But I don't have a nickname people use, and I can't get a whole new wardrobe. Should I get a life-changing haircut or something? Nothing is coming to me.

"Just wanted to make sure you're okay with it," she says. "I know how you are with change."

I *psshaw* that away, but I'm kind of glad that she gets that about me, that she knows I'm terrible with change. "You're already sophisticated, though, Ar," I remind her. "I mean, you go to the ballet every year with your mom."

She laughs. "Um, yeah, but that's because my mom buys the tickets."

"Okay, well, you're mature—I mean, you babysit for Gemma all the time, and your parents are never worried that you two are home alone and gonna burn down the house."

"Kay." She puts her hands on my knees. "I get what you're saying, I'm pretty much ready for college. So I need a name that reflects that, shows my true self."

"Okay, well, if you think of something that I can do like that, *Arianna*, just let me know." I take a lip balm/ sunscreen out of the pocket of my cover-up and rub it on my lips. "Do I have to call you Arianna, too? Or can I stick with Ari? I mean, I already know you're mature and sophisticated."

BFFs should be allowed to stick with nicknames forever. It's like some kind of rule of friendship that everyone knows and accepts.

"Well, when school starts, around other people, use Arianna, okay? Otherwise, it'll be confusing. Ya know?" She puts out her hand so I'll give her the lip balm. "Just, like, try it a few times, so you can get used to it."

"Okay, Arianna." I laugh. "Ready for the pool?"

"I'm always ready for the pool," she says, picking up her neatly packed tote. She even remembered two bottles of water and the spray sunscreen.

I grab the still-damp-from-yesterday towel from the back of the bathroom door and throw it over my shoulder.

"Ryan, we're leaving," I yell as I'm running upstairs to get my bag, trying to get him to hear me over the beeping of his video game. "Your eyes are going to bleed out of your head if you keep staring at that screen all day!"

He doesn't respond.

"Do you think my brother got a personality transplant and didn't tell me?" I ask Ari on the walk over to the pool, loosening my backpack straps. I can never get it to sit right on my shoulders; it's, like, digging into my skin. I definitely need a new one before school starts.

She laughs, sliding her sunglasses to the bottom of her nose and eyeing me suspiciously. "Can you do that? It would be kind of cool if you could, actually."

I hold on to my backpack straps. "I was kidding, but

yeah, could be cool. His crazy behavior has been going on for a few weeks now, but I've been mostly ignoring it because I just wanted it to disappear."

"A magical ability to make things like that disappear would be cool, too," Ari suggests.

"Totally!" I think about it for a second. I wonder if there's a way to do that, like really control our thoughts and calm them down. "Ryan and I used to be friends, ya know? And now he's either being a jerk to me or ignoring me."

"I think brothers are like that," Arianna explains. "Probably the more you stress about it, the more it will seem like a big deal."

I look at her, but she doesn't meet my gaze. "That's what you say about everything."

She laughs. "Yeah, because it's true." She stops walking to get a pebble out of her flip-flop. When she comes back up, she puts an arm around me. "Kay, you stress too much. You know this, right?"

I mumble, "I guess."

"And also," Ari continues, "I don't know anything about brothers. I'm just making this up. Gemma still thinks I'm the coolest. But that's because she's eight. I'm sure she'll find me annoying, eventually."

"Probably."

We get to the pool and throw our towels on our favorite lounge chairs. They're not really "ours," of course, but I call them ours because we always sit in the exact same spot, by the steps to the shallow end. It's half-sun, half-shade.

The best spot at the pool.

Ari goes to the bathroom, while I lather on more sunscreen. I'm about to jump in the water when out of the corner of my eye, I notice Tyler sitting on the lifeguard chair. I look away and spend all my energy trying to focus on making sure every dab of sunscreen is smoothed in. I examine the little tan dots on my legs and inspect my chipping pedicure.

"Hey, Kaylan," he says.

"Oh, um, hey." I pretend that I didn't see him sitting there, when I clearly did. "I didn't know you were working here. I've been here, like, every day this summer and I've never seen you."

"I'm just filling in for August," he says. "I'm still training, really. I want to work as a lifeguard when I'm in high school."

I'm not sure if a kid only a year older than me, who's "still training" to be a lifeguard, should really be watching over the pool, but who am I to judge?

"Don't look so nervous." He laughs, pulling up his shirt to mop up the sweat on his face. I try to look at him as he talks, but all I see is stomach. Tyler's stomach. It's tan, golden brown, and it's right there in front of my face. It's like I can't see anything else. "Joey's keeping an eye on me."

Joey's the director of the pool and a lifeguard, too.

"All right, well, I'll be careful not to drown," I say and then laugh, not really sure if that was funny or not.

"Good plan." He gives me a thumbs-up.

Tyler blows his whistle at some kids wrestling in the shallow end. He looks so official, the way he sits there, leaning back in the lifeguard chair, like he has it all under control. His hair is just the tiniest bit spiky. He even has the white sunscreen lines on his nose and his cheeks, but it doesn't look dorky on him. It's like he was born to be a lifeguard.

My left eye starts twitching and all of a sudden my arms are really itchy. Like really, really itchy. Am I getting a rash from this new sunscreen? I can't stop scratching my elbow.

I think I'm breaking out in hives. He's just Tyler, Ryan's best friend since pretty much forever, but I can't look at him all of a sudden. I need to focus my eyes anywhere else.

Suddenly just talking to Tyler makes me feel like I'm about to pass out.

And seriously, why is Ari taking three hundred years in the bathroom?

Finally, she gets back. "Ari." I pull her close and whisper, "This is so random, but do you think Tyler's cute?"

She looks around like she can't find him, and I nudge my head up toward the lifeguard chair to show her where he is.

"Umm. Maybe?" She shrugs, sitting down at the edge of my lounge chair. "Never really thought about it. . . . Let me look at him closer."

"No! Don't!" I hit her on the arm.

"Ouch! Kaylan!" She gives me a crooked look.

"Sorry." I feel his presence in this odd way. Like I know he's close by. It's like an itch that's so super-itchy, but I'm not allowed to scratch it.

Ari nudges her head toward mine and whispers, "I'm sorry to tell you this, because Agita Day and all, but Brooke and Lily are here."

"What? Really?" I'm completely zapped out of Tyler thoughts. I scan the pool to find them.

"Yeah, I guess they're back from camp." Ari looks over toward the deep end. "They're over there with that group of boys—Chase Selnowitz, and I know a few of those other boys from Hebrew School."

Brooke, Lily, and Kaylan. We called ourselves *Blick* for BLK (kind of a dumb name, now that I think about it) and we loved each other. We met in a baby music class, and our moms became friends, and then we became friends, and I figured it would be like that forever. But then, overnight, it just wasn't. Brooke and Lily were scooped up by the Phone Girls (I called them that because they were the first ones to get cell phones), and I wasn't scooped. I was a freezer-burned pint of ice cream, left to melt on the counter—until Ari moved to our school in fourth grade.

"Is Tamar here, too?" I ask. "Are you guys still gonna be Tamari this year?"

Tamar is Ari's Hebrew School BFF. She jokes that Tamar's the *me* of Hebrew School, since Tamar doesn't go to school with us. People need a BFF wherever they are; it's a simple fact of life.

"I think we're done with Tamari." She laughs at the name combination they made up. "Are you still jealous about that, Kay?" She side-eyes me.

"No," I groan, and look away. "God, why are Brooke and Lily back already? And is one of them going out with Chase?"

Last summer, Brooke and Lily went to the same sleep-away camp as the Phone Girls, and they just *loooooved* it. I overheard them talking about it all the time like it was the best thing ever and they were hanging out with celebrities or something.

Ari leans in close and puts her hands on my shoulders. "Come on, let's swim, it'll clear your head."

She takes my hand and leads me over to the pool, and we jump in together, holding hands, the way we always do. It's probably babyish, and I wonder if I should tell her that we should just jump in on our own from now on, or maybe even use the steps like normal, civilized people.

"They have mozzarella sticks at the snack bar today," Ari says, treading water and changing the subject entirely.

"What are the other specials?" I ask, even though eating is the last thing I want to do. My stomach is more knotted up than the rope we had to climb in gym last year. I can't think about Brooke and Lily. I can't talk to them, or ask them about camp, or anything without feeling totally embarrassed. It's easier when I pretend they don't exist.

Maybe there are things you just never get over. Like friendship endings, and your dad leaving, and who knows what else. Maybe I should make a Never Get Over list in my mind and just accept that some things need to stay there.

"Um, a turkey club and some blackberry smoothie," Ari explains. "Kay, let's race, okay? It'll be good for you. Crawl?"

I nod. "It's our best stroke, for sure." We take our places on the wall at the shallow end, and we ask Rebecca, one of the other lifeguards, if she'll tell us when to go.

Racing takes my mind off everything. For the few minutes that I'm trying to swim as fast as I possibly can, I'm not thinking about Brooke and Lily. I'm not thinking about Ryan being a jerk. I'm not even thinking about August 1 or agita or starting middle school.

My arms move back and forth like I'm an Olympic swimmer competing for the gold medal. My legs slice the water and it feels crisp and cool. My head turns to the side for a breath and I hear muffled sounds of children cheering and yelling. The water splashes behind me as I kick my feet. I turn my head again and hear the loudspeaker calling out the people who have food ready at the snack bar.

"Congrats," Ari says, all out of breath as soon as we touch the pool ledge. "I think that was your fastest yet."

"I think so, too," I say, smiling, as I catch my breath. "I feel like I could eat two full orders of mozzarella sticks after that swim."

"Go for it," Ari says, leaning back against the edge of the pool. "I wonder if those kids over there by the diving board are going to be in any of our classes. They look like they're our age, right?"

"Um, I don't think so. They look older."

"You think?" she asks. "Just because they're wearing itty-bitty bikinis?"

I glance over there, and crack up, and then look back at Ari. "Yeah, my mom would never let me wear that. Do you see how small the boobage areas are?"

Ari laughs so hard she has to dunk underwater for a second to calm down. "I actually have a bikini like that. My cousin gave it to me for a birthday gift, random. But I never wear it."

I stare at the Bikini Boob Girls and try to figure out their deal—boys and girls together like it's totally normal, and they're all best friends and hang out all the time.

Ari's still cracking up. "Boobage area! Is *boobage* a real word?"

I shrug. "No clue. It should be, right? Let's just say it a lot, and it'll become a thing."

"Boobage," I whisper to her.

"Boobage," she whispers back.

"We can't say it without laughing!"

"I know," she shrieks.

We flick water at each other, and then flip over to practice our one-armed hand stands.

So what if this stuff is babyish? We're still having fun. And at least the boobage areas of our bathing suits actually cover our, um, boobage.

If it were up to me, we'd skip middle school and live at the pool forever.

TWO

WE'RE WALKING OVER TO THE snack bar to get lunch when we hear someone say, "Ari! Hey! Over here."

We look all around, not knowing where the voice is coming from, and finally we find the person. She's so tall, with the longest legs I've ever seen. She doesn't even have her hair pulled back; it's just blowing in the breeze, but not at all in her face. And she doesn't even look sweaty! We walk over to the section of lounge chairs in the sun, near the deep end.

"Oh my God, hi," Ari says, leaning in to give the tall girl a hug.

"Ari, you look soooo tan," the girl says. "B. T. Dubs, Tamar said she was coming later."

B. T. *Dubs?* Ew.

"Oh cool." Ari smiles. "I haven't talked to her since the

end of Hebrew, when she went away to camp. How was your summer?"

Ari's voice always gets super-high-pitched when she's excited about something, and now it's just, like, normal. I'm getting the sense that Tamari really is over. Good.

"It was amazing," the girl replies. "I was on this teen tour with Phoebe, you know her, right? We had the best time."

I'm just standing there, feeling really stupid because I don't know this girl, and Ari hasn't introduced me. I shift my weight from my left foot to my right foot and then back again. Should I go to the snack bar and meet Ari there? I don't want to interrupt, but I also don't want to keep standing here, like I'm hovering on the side of their conversation.

"That's awesome," Ari says. "Oh, do you know Kaylan?" She turns to me. "Did you guys ever meet? I can't remember. Jules moved here last year; we're in Hebrew together."

"I don't think we've met," I say to the girl. Jules, I guess. "I'm Kaylan, but duh, Ari just said that."

"I'm Jules. Also, duh." She laughs. "You guys go to school together?"

Ari nods. "Yeah, are you gonna be at West Brookside? I forgot where you said you were going. Doesn't the end of Hebrew feel like so long ago?"

Jules plays with the beads on her bathing suit top. "It

totally does. I'm not going to West Brookside, I'm going to East, but some of my other friends are going there." She looks back over at them. "I'll introduce you."

I say, "Introduce us after lunch, okay? I'm staaarrrr-viiiiinnnggg." I try to imitate this line I heard in a movie once, but neither of them get the joke.

"Oh, uh, sure!" Jules bounces on her toes. "See you guys later."

She goes back to her group, and Ari and I keep walking to the snack bar, not saying anything. We overhear Jules say, "Oh, that's Ari, she's cool, she's, like, the only reason Hebrew School is tolerable."

Ari and I look at each other then and raise our eyebrows. "That's, like, a major compliment?" I tell her, trying to imitate Jules's sing-songy voice.

"I know, right?" Ari squeals.

It's a weird thing to know that your whole life is about to change really soon but have no idea how that change will affect you. I mean, I've been going to school with pretty much the same kids since kindergarten, and in just a few weeks I'll be in this giant school with a bazillion kids I don't know. Okay, maybe not a bazillion, but lots of new people. It'll feel like a bazillion. Maybe even a bazillion plus one.

"Hello, Brookside Pool!" We hear Joey scream through the loudspeaker. "I said, 'Hello, Brookside Pool!'"

A few enthusiastic pool goers yell back, "Hello, Joey!"

"That's not good enough!" he screams.

So then we all yell, "Hello, Joey!"

Ari and I laugh at ourselves and everyone else for how seriously we take the Brookside Pool rituals.

"Who is ready for Freeeeeeezzzzze Daaaannnncce?" he asks.

Oh no. Not Freeze Dance. Not now. Not when we're in such a visible spot between the lifeguards and the snack bar. We were just going to casually get our lunch, and eat on our lounge chairs, and process that whole Jules interaction.

"Ari!" I talk through clenched teeth. "Our mozzarella sticks are getting rubbery. Come on, run!"

"We never miss Joey's Freeze Dance," she says, putting an arm around me. "Come on! We're amazing at it. We were reigning champs two years in a row!"

Joey turns up the music. *Because I'm happy, clap along if you feel*—Ari and I are dancing, totally getting into it, doing the twist down to the pool pavement and back up. Slapping hands and shimmying all over the place.

The music stops and we freeze instantly.

We are Freeze Dance rock stars, and we know it. A bunch of people get called out, but we're still in. We'll make it to the final round; I know we will.

Clap along if you feel like happiness is the truth.

We grab hands and dance around in a circle for the next round. It feels like everything is okay. A blanket of calm spreads over me. And all that matters right then is Ari and me and the pool and Joey's Freeze Dance competitions.

"'Because I'm happy,'" I sing along with the music.

"Oh my God," I hear someone say as they pass us. "What are they doing?"

"They're, like, way too old to be that into Freeze Dance," another person says.

My cheeks flash red. My stomach sinks. I freeze, and not because the music shut off. I look around. They were talking about us.

I glance in their direction. The bikini boobage girls? They're whispering behind their hands.

They were definitely talking about us.

"Come on! What are you doing?" Ari yells. "We're still in this! We can win!"

I wonder if she heard what they said.

I keep dancing with Ari, but my heart's not in it. Those bikini boobage girls are watching us, leaning against the wall to the bathrooms, heads close together, whispering and laughing.

"Okay, Kaylan Terrel, sorry to say this, but you are out," Joey says over the microphone. "Good effort. Good effort."

I walk over to a lounge chair and pretend I didn't hear what those girls said, that I didn't just lose Freeze Dance.

"Sorry, Kay," Ari says, all out of breath. "Those

eight-year-olds are fierce. We'll get 'em next time. Come on, let's go get lunch."

"Did you hear what the boobage girls said?" I whisper. "They were totally making fun of us!"

"They were?" Ari crinkles her nose, looking around to find them. "I didn't hear that."

"They were making fun of us for freeze dancing," I explain. "We're too old to be that into Freeze Dance, something like that."

She looks over to where they're sitting and smooths out the sides of her cover-up. "Well, that's rude. We're so good at freeze dancing. There's no age limit for it, obviously."

She hesitates, still staring at them. Finally, she pulls my hand to get me to stand up. "Come on. I don't want to walk alone to the snack bar, and I'm really hungry now."

We walk quietly, trying to avoid eye contact with the boobage girls and their guy friends as we pass them. "Ari, um, I mean, Arianna," I say under my breath. "We cannot sprint to the entrance when we hear the ice cream truck, okay?"

She looks at me crooked. "Huh?"

"If Eddie runs out of the chocolate-dipped pops, we'll just have to deal."

"Um . . . okay." I'm not sure why it's taking Ari so long to see where I'm going with this.

"We can't make fools of ourselves anymore." I pause,

and wait for that to sink in. "Okay? We need to be normal. Try to be normal."

Ari puts her arm around me. "I get what you're saying, totally. But on the other hand, we gotta be ourselves. Ya know? People who run as fast as we can, get the best ice cream. That shows determination and dedication and athletic prowess and—"

"Okay." I laugh. "I get it. I get it." I wriggle away. I'm too sweaty to be that close to another person, even if she is my best friend.

THREE

AFTER MOZZARELLA STICKS AND ice cream, Ari and I lie out on our lounge chairs to soak up some afternoon sun. Even if I hadn't looked at a calendar, I'd be able to tell that it's August 1. The weather is screaming August. It's like a complete change from yesterday, when it felt like it was 300 degrees and 100 percent humidity.

Today, there's a breeze. The sun isn't as strong. It feels like summer isn't trying anymore, like it's tired and can't work so hard at being hot.

"Do you know when we get our schedules?" Ari asks me.

"How would I know?" I scoff, not meaning to sound so harsh. My words just come out that way.

"Maybe Ryan told you or something. . . . I don't know." She eye-bulges. "Sheesh. Kaylan, you need to calm down or we're never going to make it through the next month."

I look over at the boobage bikini girls again, and then look away.

I don't know how to calm down. That's the problem.

When I was waiting at the dentist the other day, I made a list on my phone.

Things I Am Worried (More Like Freaking Out) About
1. *Changing classrooms for every period*
2. *Cafeteria lunch tables where people can sit wherever they want*
3. *Remembering my locker combination*
4. *Learning how to use a combination lock*
5. *Sweat showing through my shorts*

Lists are great because you can check things off and feel like you're accomplishing stuff. But a worry list is a bad idea—because it makes me worry that I will never stop worrying.

"I just don't feel ready for middle school," I admit. "Maybe I need another year in elementary. Do you think I can stay back?"

Ari laughs. "Um, you got all As except for a B-plus in gym, and they don't hold people back for that." She pauses. "Here's what we need to do. We need to come up with a plan." She taps my knee to make sure I'm listening. "Like my name-change thing. Arianna just sounds

24

more middle school than Ari. We need to do more stuff like that."

I nod. I like where she's going with this. It's hard to stand still, to wait for something big to happen. It's better to take action; it's calming to take steps to prepare.

"Oh my God! Why didn't I think of this earlier?" I kick my feet against the lounge chair. "A list!"

"Kaylan, you and your lists . . ." She finishes the last drops of her iced tea.

"No, for real." I sit up. "Ari, you know lists always help me! But this is going to be a super-extreme list of only amazingness. The most phenomenal list in the history of lists!"

Ari leans over the side of her lounge chair a little to get closer to me.

I continue, "A list of all the awesome stuff we can do to be one hundred percent prepped and ready to rock middle school!"

"YES! You're totally right!" Ari claps. "This is going to be the best thing ever. Emergency sleepover tonight. My house."

"But Gemma always bugs us. Remember last time, she kept trying to sneak behind the couch and take videos of us?" I remind her. "We won't be able to focus."

"Oh, I already thought about that." She raises her eyebrows. "Gemma's sleeping at my grandma's tonight."

I high-five her. It's not that I don't love Gemma. I do.

She's super-adorable. I've always wished for a little sister, so I sometimes pretend Gemma is mine. But if Arianna and I are having an emergency sleepover to come up with a game plan, we can't be distracted.

"Perfect," I say. "This is going to be great. We have twenty-nine days to really get prepared. And the thing is, while I'm busy getting ready, I won't be fretting as much, ya know?"

"Exactly," Arianna says. "Having a game plan is always the way to go." She reaches over to get her book out of her bag. "I only have three chapters left and I'm still not totally sure I get what the book's about."

"At least you're almost done." I'm putting sunscreen on my leg in the shape of a heart to see if I can get a heart tan line when I feel someone standing over me.

I look up. It's Tyler.

"Hey," he says.

I rush to cover the sunscreen heart with my hand. "Hey."

"You know if Ryan's still home?" he asks me. "He didn't text me back."

I shrug. My heart's pounding but I smile, trying to play it cool. "No clue."

"All right. Later."

When he's gone, Ari raises her eyebrows at me.

"He's just Ryan's friend," I remind her. "He's slept over like a billion times. I mean, there are pictures of us running through the sprinkler together. I'm only wearing bathing suit bottoms. No top! How insane is that?"

"What? When?" Arianna gasps.

"Like a billion years ago, but still."

Arianna nods. "I just remembered something, actually. At the end-of-year Hebrew School party, some of the older girls were talking about him."

"They were?" My heart sinks for some reason. In a tiny little corner of my brain, I had this weird thought that Tyler was a secret that only I knew. "What were they saying?"

"I can't remember. . . . I guess that he was cute?"

"How can you not remember, Ari?" I continue with the sunscreen hearts, trying to calm down and focus on something other than Tyler or the boobage bikini girls or middle school. "That's like a major thing!"

She shakes her head. "You just asked me if he was cute for the first time today!"

"Right," I say, taking deep breaths.

We spend the rest of the afternoon on our lounge chairs. Ari finally finishes her summer reading book, while I pore over an old issue of *Seventeen* that I found near the snack bar. It claims to have all the info I need on how to "update my back-to-school style," but all their suggestions seem like they'll cost a billion dollars.

"Ready to go?" Ari asks after we hear the announcement that the snack bar is taking the last orders of the day. "I want to tell my mom you're sleeping over, clean my room, and pick up some good snacks."

"Sounds fabulous, darling."

We gather all our stuff and pack our bags. We link arms as we leave the pool and head to our houses.

We haven't even done anything yet to really prepare for middle school, but I already feel better. Like I'm on a path to greatness. I'm on my way to figuring everything out.